TRIAL BY FURY

By E. X. Ferrars

Trial
by Fury

E. X. FERRARS

DOUBLEDAY
New York · London · Toronto · Sydney · Auckland

Published by Doubleday, a division of
Bantam Doubleday Dell Publishing Group, Inc.
666 Fifth Avenue, New York, New York 10103

DOUBLEDAY and the portrayal of an anchor
with a dolphin are trademarks of
Doubleday, a division of Bantam Doubleday Dell
Publishing Group, Inc.

Library of Congress Cataloging-in-Publication Data

Ferrars, E. X.
    Trial by fury / E.X. Ferrars. —1st ed.
        p.   cm.
    "A Crime Club book."
    ISBN 0-385-24999-3
    I. Title.
PR6003.R458T75   1989
823'.914—dc20   89-7813
                        CIP

ISBN 0-385-24999-3
Copyright © 1989 by M. D. Brown
All Rights Reserved
Printed in the United States of America
December 1989
First Edition in the United States of America
BG

TRIAL BY FURY

One

The telephone rang.

Constance Lawley reached for it and said, "Yes?"

"Mrs. Lawley," a woman's voice said.

"Yes," Constance said again.

"Are you free at the moment?" the voice asked. "For another job, I mean."

"Oh dear," Constance said. "I've only just got home. I was hoping for a week or two to myself."

"Well, if you can't, you can't. How was that last job?"

"Not bad, I suppose. They were nice people. But they wouldn't eat vegetables that hadn't been organically grown or eggs that weren't free-range. They may be right about all that sort of thing, for all I know, but it did make life complicated."

"When did you get back?"

"This afternoon. And the first thing I did was buy myself a slab of fillet steak, and I'm going to have it

with some sauté potatoes and mushrooms. I couldn't
look another salad in the face. And I've got a half bottle
of Saint Emilion and I'm going to have a nice quiet
evening."

"You mean they were teetotal too?"

"Not exactly. We sometimes had a nip of dandelion
wine. It was really quite good. And they were really
very nice people, very appreciative of everything I did
for them."

What Constance Lawley had been doing for the people of whom she was talking was housekeeping for
them for a week after the wife of a retired solicitor in
the town of Bracklington, where Constance lived, had
returned from hospital after an operation for gallstones.
For the last two years, since her husband had died and
she had found her days long and empty, Constance had
been working for an institution called the Bracklington
Helpers, who supplied helpers of all sorts to people
who, through illness or old age or calamities of other
kinds, suddenly needed assistance in their houses. She
seldom worked for more than a week for anyone, but
while she did, she would cook, wash up, shop, do some
washing if that was needed, and generally keep the
house in order.

The pay was not high, but she was interested in people and inclined to like more of them than she disliked,
and the work, after all, was what she had been doing for
most of her life. She had married young a man who was
fifteen years older than herself, and they had had two
children, one of whom, Peter, was now farming in New
Zealand, and the other, Irene, a girl of twenty-nine
who, Constance thought, was old enough to know better, was doing something peculiar with a religious sect
who were given to chanting in strange tongues and
lived in a community in the East End of London.

Constance herself was sixty. She was a small, slim, vigorous woman with short, curly grey hair that had once been dark, large dark eyes in the glance of which there was a curious mixture of directness and diffidence, a smile that was usually amiable but could be sardonic, and a firm, pointed chin. Her husband had been a lecturer in economics in Bracklington Polytechnic, and as she had his pension and in her tastes was modest, the fact that the Helpers did not pay her a great deal was not of the first importance.

"What was it you wanted me to do?" she asked.

"Just another housekeeping job," the voice which belonged to Mrs. Jay, who ran the Helpers' office for them, replied. "But if you're tired—"

"Oh, I'm not tired," Constance said. "It's just that it feels nice to be at home. But if it's something urgent, perhaps I could do it. Where is it?"

"In Long Meldon."

Long Meldon was a village about ten miles from Bracklington.

"When would I have to go there?" Constance asked.

"Not until next Wednesday. Mrs. Barrow—that's the woman's name—is coming out of hospital on Wednesday morning. She's had her appendix out. There's only herself, her husband, and a grandson in the family."

"A grandson? Then she's fairly old, is she?"

"About eighty, I think."

"Isn't it very unconventional to have your appendix out at eighty? I thought it usually hit you fairly young or not at all."

"I believe that's so. Anyway, she's had appendicitis and she's being sent home on Wednesday, and her husband's about eighty too, I believe. I'm not sure how old the grandson is."

"What happened to his parents?"

"Killed in a car crash or something like that, I gathered. And the old man's been coping while his wife was in hospital, but he sounded a bit desperate on the telephone about managing to look after her once she's home. You know how quickly they push you out of hospital nowadays. Once you're no longer actually at death's door, out you go."

"It isn't a nursing job, is it, because I'm not qualified for that?"

"No, I understand she's made a perfectly good recovery; it's just that she won't be up to the job of cooking and so on for a little while and her husband thinks that a diet of baked beans might not suit her. What about it, Mrs. Lawley? Do you feel a bit tempted?"

One of Constance's failings was that she was very easily tempted to take on work of which, only a few minutes before the telephone had rung, she had felt so glad to be free. She thought of the old man and the young boy and the still frail and convalescent woman of eighty probably trying to cook for them before she was fit to do so, and she thought of her own comparative youth, being merely sixty, and all the energy that she had to spare, and that Wednesday was some days off.

"Well, perhaps I could," she said indecisively, though her mind was really already made up.

"Good, good," Mrs. Jay said. "I'm so glad. He sounded nice. He said he got the address of the Helpers from his doctor. You'll drive out there, I suppose. The address is Colonel Barrow, Riverside, Long Meldon, and the telephone number—"

"Wait a minute," Constance interrupted. "I must get a pencil and write it down . . . Yes, all right, what is it?"

"Long Meldon 850. And they'd like you to get there

about twelve o'clock, if you can manage that. Mrs. Barrow will be home by then."

"Is it a very big house?" Constance asked. "Is there any other help?"

"I'm not sure. Colonel Barrow sounded as if he and the boy had been managing on their own, so perhaps there isn't. But you'll really take it on, will you, Mrs. Lawley? I can telephone him and tell him it's fixed up, can I?"

"Yes."

"That's very good of you. Thank you so much. I can give him your number, can't I? I dare say he'll want to ring you up himself and confirm it."

"Yes, of course."

"Well, enjoy your steak."

Mrs. Jay rang off.

Constance put her telephone down and reached for the glass of sherry that she had just poured out when the telephone rang. She went through a brief spell, as was customary with her, of cursing herself for having accepted the job in Long Meldon when there were all kinds of things that wanted attention in her own house. If she did not get down to some thorough cleaning in it soon, it would begin to look squalid. For one thing, she had been promising herself for some time to dust all her books and only half an hour ago had made up her mind to start on them next day. But if she was leaving home again on Wednesday, there were a number of other things that she must see to first.

All the same, perhaps the job would be interesting. She had never worked in an army family before and was inclined to think of them as a peculiar species who might have all sorts of strange habits and prejudices as unfamiliar to her as the importance of organically grown vegetables had been. But Long Meldon was a pretty village and life there would probably be easy and peaceful.

How impossible it is to look into the future.

At eleven o'clock on Wednesday morning she set off for Long Meldon in her Mini. She had had the car for five years and kept telling herself that it would really be an economy to sell it and buy a new one before it entirely lost its value. But she was used to it and even had a kind of affection for it. Sometimes she went so far as to get estimates for other, somewhat newer second-hand cars, but when it came to the point, she could not persuade herself to write the necessary cheque. Her little dark blue car very seldom gave her any trouble and only fairly small repair bills. She had packed a suitcase after breakfast, put it in the boot, and presently drove off through the sunny summer morning.

Long Meldon had once been a village of small stone thatch-roofed cottages that straggled along a main road for a fair distance, hence its name. The cottages had once been lived in mainly by farm labourers, but now were mostly inhabited by retired professional people from Bracklington, or even from as far away as London, Manchester, Glasgow, and other points north, who had installed central heating, dishwashers, second bathrooms, and double glazing. Their front doors were painted in a variety of bright colours, and some of them had flower baskets hanging from their porches. There had once been meadows behind the cottages; but these had now been built up with bungalows and council houses, and the two old country pubs had been transformed into quite luxurious small hotels. There were a few shops and one garage. Crossing the road under the stone arch of a bridge that was in fact the oldest struc-

ture in the village was the river Meldon, a lazy stream
flowing between steep banks overhung by willows.

Constance had to stop her car and ask a passer-by
where a house called Riverside was. She was told that
she should cross the bridge, bear left, then turn into a
small lane on the right and that the house she wanted
was about a hundred yards up it. She followed these
directions and found a gate with the name Riverside
painted on it. The gate was open, and she drove through
it into a gravelled courtyard in front of a medium-sized
stone house. Stopping the car opposite the solid-looking
oak front door, she got out, took her suitcase from the
boot, went up to the door, and rang the bell.

After a moment the door was opened by a small, thin,
bearded man whose age she guessed was, as she had
been told, about eighty. In spite of his age, however, he
did not stoop, holding himself as erect as a young man,
and though his hair was white, it had receded only a
little from his high forehead. His eyes were blue, looking very bright in his deeply tanned, thin, wrinkled
face. His beard was a small one, neatly trimmed. He was
wearing an open-necked blue shirt, grey trousers, and
slightly earthy grey canvas shoes, which gave him the
look of just having come in from gardening.

He had spoken to Constance once on the telephone
two days before, confirming that she would be coming
to Long Meldon on Wednesday morning, and she knew
that he had a rather high-pitched, hurried way of speaking, which suggested to her that he was a shy man,
nervous of addressing a stranger.

"Mrs. Lawley?" he said, holding out a hand. Its grasp
felt rough, as if it was used to a good deal of hard work.
"It's so good of you to come. My wife and I are immensely grateful. It isn't that she's ill, you know; she's
quite got over the worst, only not quite the thing yet,

and I'm sure you'll be able to give her the kind of food she ought to have instead of the rather awful things that are all that I can manage. She says she doesn't mind what she has because she hasn't any appetite anyway, but I'm sure we ought to tempt her to eat, don't you think so? No, let me carry that."

He reached quickly for Constance's suitcase as she was about to pick it up. She felt, in view of his age, that she ought to carry it herself, but he grasped it firmly.

"Come along," he said. "I'll show you your room first; then you must come and meet Dorothea. I hope you'll be comfortable, though I'm afraid the room's very small and it hasn't got a television, but you must come and watch ours whenever you want to. Have you any favourite programmes that you specially like to watch? Don't hesitate to say so. While my wife was in hospital, Colin and I often watched all kinds of programmes that we'd never have thought of watching in the ordinary way, and really we sometimes found some of them quite amusing. Colin's our grandson. Of course, it's school holidays now, so he's at home, but you won't find him any trouble."

While he was chattering, he was leading Constance to the foot of a curving staircase and up it into a narrow passage. The house, she guessed, was very old. She thought that it had probably been built in the seventeenth century and perhaps had once been a farmhouse. It was not big enough ever to have been a manor, but was much larger than a cottage and had been moderately, though not lavishly, modernized. The windows that lit the passage were small, with brightly patterned curtains, and the floor of wide polished boards, with a strip of red carpet along it, was uneven. There were some thick beams in the walls.

The room into which Colonel Barrow took her was

certainly small, with only a bed in it, covered with a pretty patchwork bedspread, a built-in hanging cupboard, a chest of drawers with an attractive old mirror standing on it, and an easy chair. But opening a door which she had assumed was part of the cupboard, he showed her with a touch of shy pride that it opened into a little bathroom that she would have to herself.

"But it's perfectly lovely!" she exclaimed.

"It's all right, you'll be able to manage, you'll be quite comfortable?" he asked with a note of anxiety in his voice.

"If you'd seen some of the places I've stayed in!" she replied. "Now what can I do? I can unpack later. If you'll show me the kitchen and so on, I can start seeing to lunch."

"No, you must come down and meet my wife and perhaps have a glass of sherry with us," he said. "She isn't in bed, you know; she gets up and sits in the drawing-room, or sometimes out on the terrace, if it's warm enough. She wanted to do that today, but there's a little bit of a breeze blowing and I thought it would be better for her to stay indoors, don't you think so yourself? We don't want her catching cold."

Constance had thought the morning very beautiful, but she answered, "You may be right." She was inclined, or at any rate appeared to be inclined, to think that other people were generally right. She disagreed with other people as seldom as she could. This could lead at times, she was aware, to hypocrisy, but on the whole, it made life easier, especially when you spent as much time as she did among strangers.

The colonel had set off briskly along the passage, leading the way, then down the stairs, and across a small stone-paved hall into a bright, attractive room beside the great open fireplace of which a small, dumpy woman was sitting.

"My wife," Colonel Barrow said. "Mrs. Lawley."

He smiled at them both with the air of happily congratulating himself on having brought them together.

This he had actually done, since it had been he who had somehow cleverly discovered while his wife was still in hospital that an organization called the Bracklington Helpers existed and that they, if you were fortunate, would be able to send some kind woman to your home to look after it if you happened to be in trouble.

There were no obvious signs that Mrs. Barrow was in trouble, except for shadows under her eyes which perhaps were not normally there and a slight tightness of the mouth. But in a face as wrinkled as hers it was difficult to tell how much came from illness and how much simply from old age. Her eyes were grey and so was her hair, which was drawn straight back from her small oval face and twisted into a roll at the back of her head. She was wearing a gaily patterned cotton dress, no stockings, and velvet bedroom slippers. Her bare legs showed some prominent veins. She sat slumped on a sofa and, when Constance was introduced to her, did not move except to hold out a small hand to her and to give her a small, singularly sweet smile.

"We're so grateful to you for coming," she said. "Not that we couldn't have managed by ourselves. My husband's making too much fuss of me. I'm really very well."

"That's the problem," Colonel Barrow said. "Trying to stop her doing more than she ought. She isn't used to being ill. Now you'll have some sherry, won't you? Then we can discuss how we're going to arrange things."

"You must tell us how you like to do everything,"

Mrs. Barrow said. "We'll leave it all entirely to you. We aren't used to having a housekeeper. Of course, when we were in India before the war, we had quite a household. We had a cook and a boy and an ayah and a dhobi and a dersey and a sice, and I had absolutely nothing to do. You can't think how bored I used to get. Now we just have a very wonderful woman called Mrs. Newcome, who comes in twice a week to clean the house. She'll be coming tomorrow. You'll like her; she's so kind and efficient. But when it comes to deciding what to give us to eat, you must say what you want to cook and tell my husband what you want him to get from the shops, or he can show you where to go shopping yourself, if that's what you'd prefer."

A feeling that she was in luck and might have a pleasant week ahead of her came over Constance.

Sitting down, accepting the glass of sherry that the colonel brought to her, she said, "But you must tell me how you like things done. For instance, what do you like to eat and what don't you?"

"Oh, we eat everything," Mrs. Barrow said. "We really aren't difficult."

"No allergies?" Constance said. "Nothing I must be careful to avoid?"

"Not a thing," the old man said as if the suggestion that he or his wife might have anything so outlandish were faintly shocking. "No indeed. If you've travelled as much as we have, you can't afford to have allergies."

"Though there are some things we like better than others, that's true," his wife said. "But I don't think there's anything we couldn't eat if we had to."

"But we don't much care for tripe," Colonel Barrow said on a note of apology, as if he were afraid that Constance's only aim at the moment might be to hurry down to the butcher in the village and buy tripe in quantity.

"Nor octopus," Mrs. Barrow said. "My husband was stationed in Italy for a time after the war, and they were always giving us octopus. I could never really take to it."

"And I don't like oysters," a voice said behind Constance.

She started and looked round and saw the handsomest young boy whom she could remember ever having seen, looking gravely at her.

He had come in through the French window that opened out of the drawing-room onto a terrace where there were garden chairs placed around a round whitepainted table. There was a chessboard on the table with white and black chessmen standing about on it, as if the boy had been in the middle of a game with himself when he had stopped it to come in and take a look at Constance. The French window had a modern look and must have been pierced through the thick wall of the house not so very long ago, for it did not match the little casement on the opposite side of the room or go with the low beamed ceiling and yawning old fireplace, in which logs had been neatly laid across the firedogs, though naturally on such a fine August day they had not been lit.

The boy came forward. He was dressed in jeans and a loose white shirt.

"Anyway, you couldn't get oysters in Long Meldon even if you wanted to," he said reassuringly. "They're still alive when you eat them, you know. *Alive!* Just think of it. I'm Colin."

"Our grandson," Colonel Barrow said.

Constance could not make up her mind about the boy's age. He was about the same height as his grandfather, slender like him, and he moved with a compact kind of grace. He had black wavy hair cut so that it showed the perfect shape of his head, dark eyes, and delicately etched dark eyebrows above them. His face was narrow and thin, with a thin high-bridged nose and a mouth that was on the smallish side but with finely modelled lips. They smiled pleasantly at Constance, showing regular, very white teeth as he came forward and held out his hand to her. She had a feeling that he was aware of how his looks probably impressed her. She smiled back at him, placing him as probably twelve or thirteen years old, though perhaps rather old for his age. That might be a result, she thought, of his having been brought up by grandparents instead of parents. Yet even as she thought this, it seemed to her that there was a certain strangeness about the boy, some of it due to his astonishing good looks, but some of it to the almost fiery intensity with which he looked at her.

It was a feeling that she was to remember later.

Drinking her sherry, she suggested that Colonel Barrow should show her the kitchen and that she could then proceed to producing some lunch, what it could be depending on what happened to be in the house. Then after it, she said, she could go to the village shops to choose something for the evening.

The colonel held up a hand.

"No need," he said. "I thought that you wouldn't want to dash out shopping as soon as you got here, so the lunch, such as we're used to having, is out in the dining-room now. We never have much lunch. There's bread and cheese there and some fruit—peaches, bananas, that sort of thing—and you'll find the freezer's well stocked up with things I got from Marks and Spencer in Bracklington yesterday. I'll introduce you to the shops tomorrow."

One of the problems that Constance often encountered in her work then showed itself. It was simply the question of whether she should eat with the Barrows in the dining-room or alone in the kitchen. The Barrows took for granted that she would eat with them, but she stuck to a principle that she had worked out for herself that it was far better to insist from the beginning that she would stick to the kitchen for her meals. For warm though her welcome might be when she first arrived in a household in need of her help, they might soon become tired of her company once they were used to her. Besides, she found it restful herself to eat comfortably in silence, without having to make the effort of conversing with people whom she hardly knew. That day, when Colonel Barrow had shown her the kitchen, which she was relieved to see had been satisfactorily modernized with a dishwasher, refrigerator, and other conveniences, and when she had been up to her room once more to unpack her suitcase, she sat down at the kitchen table, ate bread and cheese, and reflected that she saw no serious problems ahead of her.

She began her work once lunch was over, clearing the dining-table and stacking the dishwasher, and then, because she had nothing special to do for the moment yet felt restless in her new surroundings, she began to make a cake. Mrs. Barrow, she knew, had gone upstairs to lie down while the colonel had gone out to work in the garden. The boy, she thought, had returned to his interrupted game of chess. But presently, while she was beating the eggs and sugar for a sponge, he appeared at the kitchen door.

"Hallo," he said diffidently, looking unsure if he would be welcome.

"Hallo," Constance replied.

"What are you doing?"

"Making a cake."

"Do you like making cakes?"

"Sometimes."

"I'm going to have a cake for my birthday."

"That sounds nice. When is it?"

"On Sunday."

"How old will you be then?"

"Fifteen."

It troubled her. She had decided that he was probably a rather sombre and dignified twelve-year-old, and now she had to think of him as a somewhat childish teen-ager.

He advanced into the kitchen.

"How long are you going to stay here?" he asked.

"A week, I think," she said.

"Do you like it here?"

"I think I'm going to like it very much."

"I don't much like it," he said. His glowing eyes had been fixed intently on her face ever since he had appeared at the door. She began to have an uncomfortable feeling that in spite of their brilliance there was a certain emptiness in them. "I've always lived here. My mother and father are both dead."

"I'm sorry," Constance said.

"You needn't be. I can't remember them. They were both killed when I was a baby."

"In a car crash?"

"Something like that."

It was said in a flat tone, as if it were a matter of no importance, yet it startled her.

"You mean you aren't sure . . ." But she stopped herself. The boy had said everything since he had come into the kitchen in the same tone and probably the matter really was of no importance to him.

"My mother was very beautiful," he said. "Everyone says so."

If he had inherited his good looks from her, Constance thought, this could well be true.

"Was she the daughter of Colonel and Mrs. Barrow," she asked, "or was your father their son?"

"Oh, she was their daughter," he said.

"Then your name isn't Barrow," she said. "What is it?"

"It's Barrow. Of course it's Barrow." He spoke with sudden excitement. "I'm Colin Barrow."

She nearly asked him if his parents had been first cousins. If they had, she thought, it might partly account for what was strange about their beautiful son, but she stopped herself, feeling that perhaps this would be getting into deep water.

"My father was no good," he announced. "Everyone says so."

"Who are everyone?"

"Oh, Grandma and Grandpa. Do you play chess?"

The change of subject was so abrupt that she was fairly sure it was what he had come to the kitchen to ask her.

"I'm afraid I don't," she answered. "I'm not nearly clever enough."

"You don't really have to be clever if you can find someone to play with who isn't a lot cleverer than you are. I play a lot with Conrad. I can generally beat him, but sometimes I think he lets me do it on purpose."

"Who's Conrad?" She was folding flour into her sponge.

"He's a friend of ours. He lives just a little way up the

lane, but he works in Bracklington. He's got a shop there."

"What kind of shop?"

"He sells furniture and things."

"Oh, Conrad Greer!" She recognized the name of one of the antique shops in an arcade in the heart of Bracklington. Most of the shops there were antique shops or bookshops or boutiques or small, expensive jewellers. She could only very occasionally afford to shop there.

Colin nodded. "Do you know him then?"

"I think I've spoken to him," she said. "I once bought a little Chelsea bowl in his shop. I suppose it would be he who sold it to me."

"He's very nice," Colin said. "I think he may be coming over to us later today because Wednesday's early closing day in Bracklington. I wish you played chess too."

"I'm sorry I don't." She slid her sponge into the oven and said, "I do hope this will be a success. It's sometimes difficult to get it right with an oven you don't know."

"I hope it will be too. Grandma's no good at cakes. Usually we just have chocolate biscuits for tea."

He gave her the first warm smile that she had seen on his face and suddenly left the kitchen.

The sponge was a success, and Constance found that dinner that evening had been so organized beforehand by Colonel Barrow that she had very little to do. She found a cooked chicken in the refrigerator and the makings of a salad and also a packet of ice-cream and a tin of peaches. Not an exhilarating meal, and next day, she promised herself, she would provide something more interesting for the family, but for a first evening in the household, when she still hardly knew where to lay her hands on what she wanted, it was certainly convenient.

The Barrows were very insistent that she should join them again for sherry before dinner, and as she could not claim that she had any more to do just then than to lay the table, she accepted. Going into the drawing-room, she saw Colin outside on the terrace, seated at the table there, poring over the chessboard on it and with a man sitting facing him who at that moment gave a laugh and said, "You've got me again. How d'you do it?"

He got up, laid a hand for a moment affectionately on Colin's shoulder, and then came through the French window into the room.

Colonel Barrow said, "Our neighbour, Mr. Greer. Mrs. Lawley." To the man he added, "Mrs. Lawley has come to look after us till Dorothea is well enough to cope again. Sherry, Conrad?"

"Thank you."

The man was the one of whom Constance had a faint recollection from the occasion when she had ventured into his shop to spend a little more than she could really afford on a small Chelsea bowl that had taken her fancy. She had often passed the shop and had paused to look at the bowl with steadily growing desire a number of times before finding herself turning almost without any intention of doing so into the shop and asking the price of it. It now stood on the mantelpiece in her sitting-room, and she was as much in love with it as ever.

She remembered that there had been a woman in the shop as well as the man, but it was he who had attended to her and she could now remember nothing about the woman. The man was tall, dark-haired, dark eyed, with thin, sharp features, wide shoulders, and a lounging, loose-limbed way of moving which is possible only to the well-muscled. Today he was wearing tan trousers and a cream shirt which looked casual yet somehow

costly. She thought that he was about forty-five or perhaps even fifty, but was someone who would always
carry his years lightly.

"Good evening, Mrs. Lawley," he said. "I'm so glad
my friends have someone to look after them. Not that
Colonel Barrow couldn't manage. He's an immensely
practical man, you'll find. But I know if Mrs. Barrow
saw him busy with the dishwasher, for instance, she'd
be itching to push him out of the way and do the job
herself, even though she ought to be taking things very
quietly." He had a slow, gentle way of speaking in a
deep voice that was softer than seemed to match the
powerful look of his tall body. "Haven't we met before,
Mrs. Lawley?"

"I came into your shop once," she answered, surprised that he should remember her.

"Ah yes, some time ago, wasn't it?"

"I should think about two years."

"As long as that?" He smiled. "It just shows how few
customers I have if I can remember for such a time the
ones who come in and actually buy something instead
of just asking if they may look around and going out
again, empty-handed."

"Conrad!" Colin called from the terrace. "Come and
play another game." He had set the chessmen up again
on the board. "And don't throw the game away like you
did last time. Come and play properly."

"No, I must go home," Conrad Greer answered. He
sipped his sherry. To the Barrows he went on, "I didn't
throw the game away, you know. The boy's getting very
good. I used sometimes to let him win on purpose, but
not any longer."

"He's so good at mathematics too," Mrs. Barrow said
and sighed as if this were something that faintly worried her. "I suppose it's good to be clever at something,

but of course he'll never be quite like other children. If only he enjoyed cricket or football or something."

"I hated them both when I was his age," Conrad Greer said. "I'm glad he's spared them at that school he goes to."

Mrs. Barrow explained to Constance, "He goes to that special school in Bracklington for—well, for handicapped children. 'Handicapped'—doesn't that sound awful? We did try sending him to the Academy, but he was miserable there. The other children realised he wasn't just ordinary and bullied him dreadfully. Yet he's so clever at some things."

"Perhaps he'll turn out a great mathematician," Conrad Greer said. "Most mathematicians are slightly mad."

"But he isn't *mad!*" she exclaimed in a horrified voice. "You don't really mean that."

"No, of course I don't—not in that sense," he replied. "I just meant a little inoffensively crazy."

"You've always been so good to him. I don't think there's anyone he cares about as much as you."

"Well, he's a lovable boy in his odd way, and one can see life's going to be hard for him."

"What I should like," Colonel Barrow said, "is to keep him at home and have a tutor for him, but we couldn't possibly afford that. So it's a choice between the special school, where he doesn't really belong, or a common-or-garden public school, where he'd be miserable. Of those two I prefer the special school. In another year, anyway, he can leave school, and perhaps we can manage to get him some coaching which might get him into a university if his maths are really as good as they say."

"Or perhaps he'll do some growing-up, given time. It's his birthday one day soon, isn't it?"

"On Sunday," Mrs. Barrow said. "We've ordered a cake from Jennifer."

Greer finished his sherry. He turned back to Constance.

"You won't have met Jennifer yet, Mrs. Lawley," he said, "but I'm sure you will. She's something special. She runs a little café in the village where the cakes are home-made and actually eatable and the coffee's excellent. A nice girl too. You must ask Colonel Barrow to take you there to meet her."

"Mrs. Lawley made us a sponge-cake for tea which was delicious," Mrs. Barrow said as if she were coming in a hurry to Constance's defence. "Of course, Jennifer is a professional, but I can tell already we're very lucky to have got Mrs. Lawley to come to us."

"Of course you are."

Greer stooped and kissed Mrs. Barrow on the cheek, smiled at Constance, and went out on to the terrace again—his usual way, she supposed, for getting to his home.

That last glance of his had taken Constance to some extent by surprise, for it seemed to her that for a moment his eyes, with a probing shrewdness in them, were assessing her with what was almost distrust. Perhaps it was not to his discredit that he should want to make sure that in fact the two old Barrows were really as fortunate as they had leapt to the conclusion that they were in having her to look after them, that she was not likely to extort money from them by devious means or make off with the silver. Yet there was something chilling about the brief look that he had given her, though when he had gone, she quickly forgot about it. When she thought of him later, she remembered only how kind he had seemed to be to that odd boy, Colin.

If she had been twenty years younger, she thought,

she would probably have found the man very attractive. Being sixty, she saw this quality in him with what was really a very comfortable feeling of detachment. There was no challenge in it, no sense that she ought to be provoked into competition with anybody else. There were certain compensations, after all, in growing old.

Next day she had a talk about Colin with Mrs. Newcome, the woman from the village who came in twice a week to clean the house. She was a tall, bony woman of about fifty with a long, lugubrious face and not much desire to gossip. On arriving, she immediately extracted the vacuum cleaner from its cupboard and went to work, recognizing Constance's presence in the kitchen only by a terse greeting and the observation that it wasn't as fine as it had been yesterday and that she wouldn't be surprised if there was rain before evening. She was dressed in trousers which fitted her gaunt figure admirably and a brightly spotted red-and-white shirt. Her thick grey hair was stylishly arranged, as if she had just come from the hairdresser.

Presently, about half-way through the morning, she sat down with Constance for a cup of coffee. Some time before that, Constance had taken breakfast up to Mrs. Barrow, who had told her gratefully that breakfast in bed was one of the luxuries of life that she most enjoyed and had exclaimed at how good of Constance it was to have struggled upstairs with the tray. Colonel Barrow and Colin had had coffee and toast and marmalade in the sunshine on the terrace; then the colonel had gone off to work in the garden, and what Colin was doing Constance did not know.

She said to Mrs. Newcome that it seemed to her that the Barrows were particularly nice people.

"That's right," Mrs. Newcome said. "I've been working for them ever since they came here and that's twelve years ago or more, so I should know. They don't criticize, don't interfere with you, just let you get ahead with your work, and generous too. Give a good deal to things in the village, though they don't mix in much. I suppose they like a quiet life after all the travelling around the world they had to do, him being in the army and being posted from one place to another—India, Italy, Cyprus, Malaya, and then living in Bracklington for a time after he retired from the army and went into business of some sort there. Never had a real home of their own till they come here. It was for the sake of the boy they done that. Of course, he was only a tot when they come; you couldn't tell how he'd turn out."

"Then his parents were dead already?" Constance said.

"That's right. Killed in a car crash on one of those motorways. My husband won't drive on a motorway if he can help it. He's a decorator and works for a firm of builders in Bracklington, but he does a bit of gardening for people hereabouts when he's got some spare time. He looks after Mr. Greer's garden for him. He's a neighbour of Colonel and Mrs. Barrow."

"I met him yesterday evening," Constance said. "He runs an antique shop in Bracklington, doesn't he?" Remembering vaguely the woman whom she had seen in the shop on the occasion when she had gone into it, she asked, "Is he married?"

"No, he lives alone. Well, I say alone. That's most of the time." Mrs. Newcome made a grimace which might have been taken for a rather lewd wink. "He's a good-natured sort of man, I'll say that for him. Says he's sure the boy's going to turn out all right in the end."

"He's a nice boy, isn't he?" Constance said. "Perhaps

he's just what I believe they call a late developer. He seems very friendly."

"Ye-es," Mrs. Newcome said after a slight hesitation. "Yes, he's all right most of the time. Can be as nice as can be when he feels like it. But you want to look out with him; he's got a terrible temper. I've seen him shriek and storm and break things. I'm always very careful with him."

They were both startled by the sound of the kitchen door slamming. Beyond it they heard the sound of running feet. A moment before the door had stood open. Now it was closed.

"There," Mrs. Newcome said, "you see what I mean. I believe he was standing there, listening to what I was saying. I'm a fool. For all I know, that's pushed him into one of his terrible rages."

Two

When Constance next saw Colin there was no sign that
he was in a rage or had been in one. It seemed to her
that he was a little more aloof than he had been before
and that his brilliant eyes, instead of dwelling on her
face, avoided looking directly at her, but that might
have been imagination on her part because she was
watching for indications that he was upset. If he was
angry with anyone, it was with Mrs. Newcome. Once
she had left the house, he came into the kitchen and
offered to help Constance lay the table for lunch. As it
had been yesterday, it was only bread and cheese and
fruit, and before it Colonel Barrow came out, as he had
before, and insisted that Constance should join his wife
and himself for sherry.

When the bread and cheese had been eaten and the
table cleared and Mrs. Barrow, saying apologetically
that she could not understand why she got so tired

when she had done absolutely nothing, had gone upstairs to lie down, he suggested that Constance might
like to go to the shops in the village with him and see if
there was anything that she would like to buy for the
evening.

"We could walk, if you feel like it," he said, "or we
can drive, if you'd sooner. I like the walk myself and it
isn't far."

"Let's walk," Constance said. "I'd like to get to know
the village."

"It's a pleasant place," he said. "We've lived here for
some time now. We lived in Bracklington for a while
after I retired from the army. I had a job as personnel
director with Robert's and White's, but when Colin was
left on our hands, I gave it up and we moved out here
because we thought it would be a better life for him. He
likes you, incidentally. You can see that, can't you? It's
lucky, because between you and me he can be a little
devil if he doesn't like a person. I don't know where he
gets it from. His mother was a very quiet girl, almost too
quiet, I sometimes used to think. Never cared much to
play with other children and never wanted anything
but to play the piano. Perhaps that was the trouble, I
mean why Colin's not exactly—well, an ordinary boy.
He may have inherited something from her. Her mother
and I used often to worry about her."

"What did her husband do?" Constance asked.

"Who? Oh, her husband. Oh well, he was in business. In Bracklington too, you know; that's where they
met."

That seemed to be all that he intended to tell Constance about his daughter's husband. As being "in business" is one of the vaguest descriptions that can be
given of anyone and as the colonel's voice had become
suddenly brusque when he replied to Constance's ques-

tion, she deduced that he had had no great liking for his son-in-law. She wondered if he had been driving when the car in which he and his wife had lost their lives had crashed and if her parents blamed him for her death.

Presently the colonel and Constance set off together for the shops. Mrs. Newcome's prophecy that there would be rain before the evening looked as if it might come true. Clouds were beginning to pile up across the sky, blotting out some of the brightness of the sunshine, though in between them it shone brightly on the quiet countryside. The walk along the lane to the main road, then over the bridge, and into the straggling village took only about a quarter of an hour. Colonel Barrow walked briskly, holding himself as erect as ever and carrying a walking-stick in one hand and a shopping basket in the other. As they walked, he started to ask Constance questions about her work, about the other people to whom she had been sent at different times, and about her family. She spoke freely about her son, farming in New Zealand, but felt embarrassed at talking about her daughter. Could this kindly man understand a young woman who had chosen to live on unemployment pay in a community in the East End of London which indulged in vague good works in the inner cities, worshipped some strange god, and for relaxation went in for a great deal of chanting? Constance could not understand it herself.

But the colonel seemed to have a fair understanding of his grandson, so perhaps the girl's eccentricities would not seem too incomprehensible to him after all.

The first shop at which they stopped was a butcher's, where Constance chose a leg of lamb and some bones from which to make stock. Colonel Barrow did not pay for them, but had them put on his account. He told her that if she was shopping by herself during the next few days, she need pay for nothing, as he had accounts everywhere. From the butcher they went on to a shop that was mainly a grocer's, but which also stocked fruit, vegetables, drink, cigarettes, newspapers, women's tights, and a remarkable range of frozen food. It was a very modern, self-service shop, and it would have been possible, Constance thought, looking round it, in spite of its being quite as small as village grocers used to be, to depend on it entirely for all one's needs.

She bought potatoes, a cauliflower, and some raspberries and cream, all of which went into the colonel's basket. She kept noticing other things that she would have liked to buy, but was afraid that the basket would become too heavy for him. They were just about to leave the shop when someone called out, "Godfrey, darling!" and it appeared that Godfrey darling was the colonel. He turned and smiled at a young woman who had just come up behind them.

She darted at him and kissed him on the cheek.

"You must come over and have a cup of coffee," she said. "You will, of course."

"We've only just been drinking coffee at home," he said.

"Well, have a little more. You must. I haven't seen you for ages."

"Not since last week," he said. "Mrs. Lawley, this is our friend, Jennifer Hyland, the one we were telling you about who makes the splendid cakes. Jenny, this is Mrs. Lawley, who's come to look after us till Dorothea gets better."

The young woman smiled at Constance and said, "Hallo." Then she asked, "How is Dorothea?"

She looked about thirty and was short and somewhat stocky, with curly fair hair cut short and brushed forward over a low forehead, a broad face on which there was no make-up, big grey eyes, and a wide, good-humoured mouth. She was wearing a sleeveless dress of dark green cotton and bright red sandals on her bare feet.

"She's doing pretty well," Colonel Barrow said. "Why don't you come up and see her?"

"I will, I will, as soon as I've a spare moment, I promise. I've been busy making some things that have been ordered as well as that cake for Colin. That's got to be a work of art, of course. I'll bring it up myself and have a chat with Dorothea then. Now do come across and have some coffee."

"But if you're so busy . . ."

"Oh, never too busy for my friends. And I've got everything I want here. I only popped across to buy some eggs. I suddenly found I was running out of them." She turned to Constance. "You'll come, won't you?"

Naturally, they went.

Jenny's Café, as it was called, was just across the road, opposite to the grocer's. It was a thatched cottage with beams in its white walls and at some time had had a very inappropriate curved bay window let into its frontage beside a door that stood open. Through the window, Constance saw small round tables covered with checked cloths and set with cups and saucers.

Jennifer Hyland took them into the room with the bay window, where a few customers were having either a late lunch or an early tea, waited on by a brisk little woman in a pink overall, and through the room to a garden behind the cottage, where more small round tables under wide umbrellas were dotted about a lawn. Setting Constance and the colonel down at one of the tables, she said that she would be back with the coffee in a moment and darted away. She did everything quickly, with a look of exuberant vigour.

"She's a dear girl," Colonel Barrow said, "and making a great success of this place, which I never thought she would when she started it. It's only been going for a couple of years. Conrad Greer found the cottage for her, just as he found our house for us. Her sister, Julie, works for him. Very interesting girl, Julie, but she and Colin don't hit it off—don't ask me why. Sometimes I think he may be a bit jealous of her, working for Conrad. Wasn't Dorothea saying yesterday that he worships Conrad, and I don't think Colin likes him to care for anyone but himself. Absurd, of course, but that's what some children are like. They don't realise that other people have lives of their own."

"Here we are, my dears." Jennifer was back in the garden with cups of coffee on a tray. "Now tell me all about yourselves, and tell me, do you want candles on Colin's cake?"

Her sister, Julie, Constance thought, must be the woman of whom she had a dim recollection in Conrad Greer's shop when she had bought her Chelsea bowl. There had been something very pleasant about that occasion, a feeling that the man congratulated her on having spotted one of the best things in the shop, even if a number of other things were more expensive. All that it had meant, of course, was that he was a very good salesman, but a sense that she would like to go back to the shop simply to meet him again had remained with her for a while. Then she had forgotten about him until she had met him the evening before.

"Candles, dear me, yes," Colonel Barrow said. "I'm sure Colin wouldn't feel it was the real thing without candles. And fifteen isn't so very many, is it? I mean, there'll be plenty of room for them. I can't remember when I stopped having candles on my birthday cakes. I suppose it was when I went into the army, because my birthday had a way of happening when I was in all sorts of God-forsaken places and I'd started thinking in terms of champagne, if that was possible, rather than cake. Then Dorothea and I started having birthday cakes again after we came here, but that was to amuse Colin. And we'd have just one candle standing in the middle of the cake and we'd let him blow it out and make a wish."

"You've always been so wonderful with that boy," Jennifer said, "but I find it very difficult to remember he's fifteen. I know Conrad says in some ways he's very clever, but he seems such a child."

A shadow of sadness passed across Colonel Barrow's face.

"Oh yes, and I suppose it's probable he'll never grow up. We've taken him to three psychiatrists, you know, and they all say he's got a very high IQ and he could catch up with other children quite easily if he wanted to. Only he just doesn't seem to want to. I know that's how it was with him with reading and writing. He simply wouldn't try to read until he was about seven, and then all of a sudden there was nothing else he wanted to do and he could do it at once. We sometimes feel, you know, Dorothea and I, that it must be our fault. If he'd had a normal family life instead of coming to live with two such old people, we think he might not have clung so hard to being a baby."

"Of course you've spoiled him terribly," Jennifer said, reaching out and patting Colonel Barrow's hand with reassuring friendliness. "Terribly. But that's what grandparents are for, isn't it? That's what our own were like to Julie and me. They let us get away with anything. We adored them." She turned to Constance. "Julie's my sister. She works in Conrad's shop."

"So Colonel Barrow was telling me," Constance replied.

"She really knows much more about antiques than he does. In the ordinary way she'd probably have been here this afternoon, because it's early closing in Bracklington, but she's gone to a sale in Oxford and I don't suppose she'll get home till the evening. She lives with me, but I don't see very much of her. She won't have anything much to do with the café. She thought I was mad to try to make a go of such a thing. But I thought she was mad to go into the antique trade. Sisters don't really know the first thing about one another, do they? Our parents wanted us both to be scientists or teachers or something like that and lavished education on us, first an awfully good, dreary sort of girls' school, then Julie went to Cambridge and I went to Edinburgh, and after all that, she became a shop assistant and I took to cooking. Have you always done the sort of work you do now?"

"In a way, yes," Constance said. "That's to say, I've just lived a more or less domesticated life. But then when my husband died and both of my children went away I felt I'd got to do something or I'd simply become a vegetable, and it happens that the sort of work I've been doing is the only kind I'm qualified to do."

"What are your children doing?" Jennifer asked.

"Peter's joined a friend of his who's bought a farm in New Zealand," Constance answered, "and I think he's doing very well. And Irene—well, she's taken to a sort of social work."

It was the best that she could do to describe Irene's peculiar activities without risking the embarrassment of having to explain what these were. The term "social work" fortunately was generally accepted as covering a multitude of strange goings-on.

"Does she live in Bracklington?" Jennifer asked.

"No, in London," Constance said.

"But you live in Bracklington yourself, don't you?"

"Yes."

"Then perhaps you know Conrad's antique shop."

"I do, as a matter of fact."

"The trouble is, he's such a snob about antiques, and Julie's got just like him. If you buy something you just happen to think is pretty and you pay what you think you can afford, they'll start pointing out to you that some repair work's been done on it and it isn't really all genuine, as you were told, and it's got a few worm holes or something and that you've paid twice too much for it. Since Julie's come to live with me, I've stopped buying anything that isn't obviously and unashamedly modern; then she can't spoil it for me."

The tone was cheerful, yet something gave Constance a feeling that the two sisters might have been wiser not to try to live together. She said as much to Colonel Barrow when presently he and she started on their way back to Riverside.

"Have Julie and Jennifer been living together for long?" she asked. "It sounds to me as if it might be a rather uneasy relationship."

"Well, they are very different, that's true," he said, "but I'm sure they're very fond of one another. When we knew them first, we thought for sure Julie and Conrad were going to get married. That was some years ago, but nothing came of it. Whether or not there's been a— well, a relationship—" He broke off, giving a slight scowl which Constance thought was directed at himself. "You see what it does to one, living in a place like Long Meldon. One turns into a terrible old gossip, there's so little else to talk about. It's worse than the army."

"I think it's going to rain," Constance said. "Perhaps we ought to hurry."

The sky had become quite overcast and a wind had started up which made the leaves of the chestnuts that lined the village street toss against one another.

"Yes," Colonel Barrow said, "yes indeed. We mustn't have you getting wet and catching cold. We'd really be in trouble then, shouldn't we?"

Holding his walking-stick and the shopping basket, he started to stride along faster.

But as Constance felt the first drops of rain on her face, a voice hailed them.

"Hallo, Godfrey! Hallo, Mrs. Lawley!"

It was Conrad Greer.

Colonel Barrow said, "What are you doing here at this time of day, Conrad? Oh, of course, it's early closing in Bracklington."

"I was going to say, in another minute or two you'll be soaked," Greer said. "I've got my car here. Shall I drive you home?"

"Now that would be really kind," the colonel said.

"Wait a minute, then, I'll get it." Greer strode off to where his car was parked.

In a minute or two he was back with it. The rain was already gathering force. Constance was glad that she would not have to walk through it all the way back to Riverside.

"How's Dorothea?" Greer asked as the three of them got into the car.

"Doing quite nicely, I think," Colonel Barrow replied.

"In that case, I mean if you aren't in a hurry to get back to her, why not come home with me? I've something I'd like to show you."

Colonel Barrow looked questioningly at Constance. "We could do that, couldn't we?"

"Of course, if you want to," she replied.

"All right then—thank you, Conrad. Only don't offer us coffee, or tea either, for that matter. We had coffee at home, then some more with Jenny, and when we get home, Dorothea will be wanting tea."

"I won't even offer you a drink," Conrad said, "we English having been conditioned to think it's impossible to consume alcohol between three and half past five in the afternoon."

"But surely it *is* impossible." The colonel looked troubled. "Isn't it? Or is that really just this conditioning you're talking about?"

"Well, the French do it," Greer said. "I think even the Americans sometimes."

"Is that so?" It seemed to be news to Colonel Barrow. "Come to think of it, in India I used to have my whisky and soda at all sorts of odd times of the day. But that was because of the climate, of course. It upset all one's old habits. What do you want to show us, Conrad?"

"Wait and see. I'd like your opinion on it. I mean, if it's, well, suitable."

"It's something for Colin's birthday, is it?"

"Yes."

"You're always so good to him. I hope you haven't been too extravagant. I'm giving him a camera myself— not a grand one, just one of the kind you can get a print off straight away. I think he'll enjoy that more than having to wait while his film's developed."

"I haven't got anything for him, but I'd like to give him something," Constance said. "Perhaps there'll be time for me to pop into Bracklington tomorrow and pick something up."

"Oh, you mustn't bother," Colonel Barrow said. "He won't expect it."

"But I'd like to. Birthdays are so important at his age."

"Well, if you really would . . . Conrad, Jenny told us Julie's gone to a sale in Oxford today. Is she after anything special?"

"Yes, there's some good Spode in the sale. An unusually complete set and one of the rarer designs. But, of course, she'll keep her eyes open for anything else at all promising."

"I wonder where you'd be without her."

"So do I sometimes. Every time she picks up with a man, I shake in my shoes. She'll get married some time, I suppose, and I'll have to look for a substitute, but I don't look forward to it."

"Why not marry her yourself; then you can stop worrying?"

Greer laughed. "If I haven't, you don't think it's for want of trying, do you?"

Colonel Barrow did not reply, and Constance believed that that was precisely what he did think though he would not dream of saying so.

The car had turned into the lane that led to Riverside, but on reaching it, Greer drove straight past the gate and did not stop until they were about a quarter of a mile further on, outside a small square house of dull red brick that had sash windows, a graceful fanlight above a white front door, and a grey slate roof. She supposed it was Georgian. It had no front garden but faced directly on to the lane, and a wooden shed to one side of it was the only structure in sight that might be a garage.

Greer jumped out of the car and opened the door for Constance. Then he unlocked the white front door and gestured to her to enter quickly out of the rain, which by now was heavy. He did not trouble to lock the car. The colonel reproved him for this, telling him that it was not fair to the police to be so casual.

Greer laughed again and said, "Who's going to come along a lane like this and bother to steal a car as old as that. But I've got good locks on all my doors and windows and some alarm bells too, because it might get around that I sometimes have valuables here. Apart from that, do you know that more people are killed in their own homes than even on the roads? It's true that most people spend more time in their homes than anywhere else, so the statistics may not mean much—" He stopped abruptly.

He had just recalled, Constance thought, that the colonel's daughter had been killed in a crash on a motorway.

"Well, come in here," Greer went on after a momentary pause, "and tell me what you think of what I've got for Colin."

He led them into a medium-sized room opening off the small hall. It had sash windows at either end of it, a small, elegant fireplace, a great many books, and rather more furniture than it really needed for comfort. There was no sign of central heating having been installed, and Constance remembered having been told that central heating was death to antiques. It might be a chilly place in winter, but if the rain had not been drumming on the windows now, it would have been a bright and cheerful room.

"Here it is," Greer said. "I picked it up at a sale in Bracklington a week ago. Chinese, of course."

What he was pointing to was a set of chessmen of red and white ivory standing on a small table. They were taller than usual, and the country of their origin was plainly to be seen in their finely carved Mongolian features. The knights were in elaborate armour; the kings and queens wore strange, lofty headgear.

"What do you think of it?" Greer asked.

Colonel Barrow did not look too sure. "They're beautiful, of course, and if they aren't wasted on him . . . You know, he doesn't care for change. Of course he'll be delighted with them and he'll set them up and sit and gloat over them, but then he may put them away in a cupboard and go on playing with the old set."

"Oh, he mustn't do that," Greer said. "These are meant to be played with."

"But don't be disappointed if that's what he does."

"Then tell him he shouldn't. Tell him I'll be very upset if he does. Tell him I won't come and play with him any more if he doesn't use them."

"Yes, I can do that," Colonel Barrow said, "and perhaps it won't be necessary. I can never tell with Colin. I'm not clever with him, you know, like you. Perhaps he won't like my camera because he's set his heart on the most expensive thing on the market. He doesn't understand about money."

" 'It droppeth as the gentle rain from heaven upon the place beneath,' " Greer said.

"That's about it. But talking of rain, Conrad, are you going to drive us home?"

"Yes, of course."

"These chessmen must have been horribly expensive. I do hope he'll appreciate them."

"If he doesn't, he can give them back to me and I'll sell them. You're sure you wouldn't like some tea or coffee?"

"No thank you."

"Then come along."

"But I'm sure he'll love them," Constance said. She

had stopped over the table to look more closely at the delicate carving of the chessmen. It worried her that Colonel Barrow should have been so discouraging to the other man. She could tell that he was hurt. "Anyone would love them, even if they never played chess in their lives."

"I know what Godfrey means," Greer said. "And it won't break my heart if they're a failure."

The drive to Riverside took only a few minutes. As Greer drove off after leaving Constance and the colonel and their shopping basket at the door, he followed her into the house and then, as she went to the kitchen, went into the drawing-room, saying, "Dorothea?" But immediately he came out again.

"She's still lying down," he said. "I'll go and call her. You'll be getting tea, won't you? I don't know where Colin is."

When Constance had made tea and put it with cups and saucers and the remains of her sponge on a tray and carried it into the drawing-room, she found that Mrs. Barrow had come downstairs and was sitting in her usual place on the sofa beside the great fireplace, but there was no sign of the boy.

"I think he's in his room," Mrs. Barrow said. "I heard him come upstairs. Perhaps he's fallen asleep. If you'd be so kind as to go up and see if he's there . . ." She looked up at Constance. "He may be reading and not want to bother with tea. You see, when we're here by ourselves and haven't you to look after us, we don't usually have tea. I've a feeling, you know, that I haven't been looked after so well since I was a child. We always had tea then, of course, with hot buttered toast or crumpets, and cucumber sandwiches and a wonderful currant cake that our dear cook used to make."

"What about India?" Constance said. "Didn't you have a whole staff of servants there to look after you?"

Mrs. Barrow looked a little embarrassed, probably at Constance having classed herself with a staff of servants when the old woman's instinct was to treat her simply as an unusually helpful guest. "They didn't understand about crumpets."

"I must see if I can buy some in the village tomorrow," Constance said. "And I'll go upstairs now and see if Colin is in his room."

She found Colin in his bedroom, which was on the top floor of the house. He was lying on his bed, neither reading nor sleeping. His eyes were wide open, staring intently at some point on the ceiling above him. She thought that he was deep in some daydream and that he did not welcome being interrupted.

"In case you're interested, I've just taken in the tea," she said.

He turned his head slowly on his pillow till his wide eyes, without having blinked, had become fixed on her face.

"Go away," he said softly.

She did not answer, but withdrew, closing the door. But before she had reached the top of the stairs, the door had been flung open and he had come charging out.

"I didn't mean that!" he shouted at her.

"All right, then comb your hair and go down and have some tea," she said.

"Yes, yes, of course I will, but I didn't mean to be rude to you." He thrust his hands through his dark curly hair, making it look even more unruly than it was already. "I didn't think you'd really go away. Usually they don't."

"Who don't?"

"Oh—people."

She felt a faint chill up her spine. Did the boy see people who were not there? And if he did, what kind of people were they? Not that that was particularly important; it was only the question of whether or not they were there that mattered.

"There's still some sponge-cake left," she said, "if you like it."

"Oh, that's super. I'll be down in a minute."

He shot back into his room, and a moment after she had reached the bottom of the stairs, with his hair neatly combed, he came bounding down them and into the drawing-room, slamming the door behind him.

Constance went into the kitchen and began unpacking the shopping basket that Colonel Barrow had left on the table there.

Presently he carried the tea-tray out to the kitchen. In spite of her insistence that she would do it, he stacked the cups and saucers in the dishwasher.

"You won't say anything to Colin about those chessmen, will you?" he said.

"Of course not," she said. "Birthday presents have to be a surprise."

"What I mean is, I'm going to try to persuade Conrad not to give them to him. They're too valuable."

"Won't Colin take care of them?"

"I expect so. Probably, but sometimes . . . The fact is, one can never be quite sure. Sometimes he can be very destructive, and something as good as those chessmen is a responsibility. I realise that Conrad, being in the trade, may not have paid nearly as much for them as you or I would in a shop; all the same, he'd be very upset if Colin took it into his head to break their heads off. I remember a time—of course he was much younger then—when he had a teddy bear he specially loved, and one day he got hold of one of my razor blades and cut it all to pieces. And there've been a few other incidents . . ." He closed the dishwasher and turned to look at Constance with a slight frown. "I wouldn't say this to most people, but I've a feeling you understand more than some would. D'you know, sometimes that boy really frightens me. I don't believe he cares in the least for his grandmother or me. I don't know what he does care about. He seems to live in a private world that we're all to keep out of. I think he cares more for Conrad than for anyone, yet there are times when I get the feeling that he hates even him. It's very strange."

"It must be very difficult for you and Mrs. Barrow," Constance said.

"Well, we've done our best, and if things haven't worked out quite as they should . . . Oh, I expect we worry too much. If we've made mistakes, we've always meant to do all we could for the boy. Things may sort themselves out as he gets older."

He left the kitchen, but for once, as he went out, his shoulders looked more stooped and his back less straight than usual.

Constance started peeling potatoes to roast around the leg of lamb, and turned on the oven.

It was about six o'clock and she had just put the joint into the oven when the doorbell rang. She did not think that answering the door was one of her duties and did not go to it, but as she did not hear any footsteps crossing the hall and as after a moment the bell rang again, she thought that perhaps it was expected of her by the Barrows that she would open the door, and she went out to it.

She saw a woman standing on the doorstep with a suitcase beside her, while a taxi was just disappearing out of the gravelled forecourt. The rain was still falling steadily and there was a cool, fresh scent of wet earth in the air.

The woman stared at her in a puzzled way and said, "Who are you?"

She was about forty, slender, tall, dark-haired, with a thin tanned face in which her pale grey eyes looked peculiarly vivid. She was wearing a raincoat with the collar turned up around her thin neck and had a bulky bag slung over one shoulder.

"I'm the help," Constance said. "Is it Mrs. Barrow you want?"

"The help?" the woman said. "Do you mean you work here?"

"For the moment," Constance replied. "Mrs. Barrow's been ill and I've come to look after things for her. Do you want me to announce you?"

"That won't be necessary." There was a curious twang in the woman's voice that Constance could not identify. All at once, picking up her suitcase, the woman pushed her way past Constance into the hall. "They know me. But I don't know this house. It's new since my time." Suddenly she raised her voice. "Hallo! Hallo! Is anybody there?"

The door of the drawing-room burst open, and Colonel Barrow came dashing out. For an instant he stood still, staring incredulously at the woman, then he took a swift step forward and clasped her in his arms.

"Margot!" he cried. "Oh my God, Margot!"

She clung to him as tightly as he to her.

"Yes, it's Margot," she said with a sob in her voice. Constance saw the gleam of tears in her eyes. "Oh, say you're glad to see me. Say it, say it!"

"Yes, I'm glad, my darling, I'm so glad!" Then he half turned away from her and shouted over his shoulder, "Dorothea, it's Margot!"

Looking even paler than usual and unsteady on her feet, Mrs. Barrow appeared in the drawing-room doorway. She held out her arms, and the woman whom Constance had just let into the house let go of the old man and went into his wife's embrace. They kissed and clung to one another; then Mrs. Barrow took hold of the other woman by the shoulders and held her a little away from her.

"This is so wonderful," she said, "but why didn't you tell us you were coming? It's almost too much of a surprise. Is Kenneth with you?"

"No, I'm alone."

"It's just a visit, is it, or . . . have you come to stay?"

"We can talk about that later. But I can stay now, can't I?"

"Of course, of course. Only . . ." Colonel Barrow glanced behind her. "What are we going to tell Colin?"

"Why not the truth at last?"

"Is that what you really want?"

"Perhaps. I don't know. We'll talk about that later too. Where is my son?"

At that moment Colin appeared behind his grandmother. Constance thought that he had been there from the first when the mother and the daughter who had supposedly been dead for years had embraced and that he had heard all that had been said. His big dark eyes, which could look so fiery or so dull and empty, were blazing as he stared at the strange woman.

"You're not my mother," he said in a quiet, flat tone. "I know you're not."

"I am," she said shakily, "You're Colin . . ."

"You're not!" he suddenly shouted. "You're not real, you're one of *them*, you're dead!"

He turned and vanished into the room behind him.

There was a crash as something on the terrace, perhaps the table with the chessmen on it, was overturned; then he must have fled into the garden, for there was silence in the room.

Three

Constance went into the kitchen and closed the door behind her. She ought to have done this sooner, she supposed, but uncontrolled curiosity had kept her where she was in the hall. Reappearance from the dead is not an everyday occurrence. She had felt unable to move. But she could not be welcome there. She had begun to divide the raspberries that she had bought in the afternoon into three glass bowls that she had found in a cupboard when she realised that they would have to be divided into four. That was supposing that the newcomer would be staying for dinner. She had arrived with a suitcase, so it looked as if she intended to stay.

If she did, a room would have to be made ready for her. Constance wondered if anyone would come out to the kitchen with instructions for her or if she would be driven into going into the drawing-room to ask what was to be done. Meanwhile, she laid the table in the dining-room for four people.

As she went to and fro across the hall, she could hear voices in the drawing-room, quiet voices, no longer excited, but she did not hear Colin's. If he was still out in the garden, he must be soaked to the skin by now unless he had found somewhere to hide. She thought of going out to look for him herself and trying to persuade him to come in, but she was afraid that if his grandparents had not already done this themselves, they might see it simply as an impertinent intrusion on her part. Opening the oven door, she basted the leg of lamb, turned over the potatoes around it, and then put the cauliflower on the stove to cook.

She had just done this when Colonel Barrow came into the kitchen.

"Please, will you come and join us in the drawing-room for a glass of sherry?" he said. "We want you to meet our daughter. And we apologize— Well, perhaps I needn't actually do that; you'll know what I mean. But we want to explain this thing, which I expect you think is really rather extraordinary."

"There's really no need, Colonel Barrow," Constance said.

"Oh, there is," he said. "Of course there is. I mean, we've lied to you about her, haven't we, and it must all seem very strange to you? And there's the problem of Colin. He'll expect you to know all about it, and we've got to decide what to say to him."

"Is he still outside?" she asked.

"Yes, but he's probably sheltering somewhere, in the tool-shed perhaps. And I think we ought to have talked the whole thing over before we go looking for him. Come along now, and meet Margot. We've explained to her who you are and what you're doing here. We hadn't written to her about Dorothea's illness, so she was rather puzzled at first. We have been writing to one another occasionally during these past years, but naturally we didn't want to send her any worrying news."

He opened the door into the drawing-room.

The first thing that Constance noticed was that she had been right: it had been the table with the chessmen on it that Colin had overturned on the terrace in his flight into the garden. The woman whom she had let into the house a little while ago was standing at the French window, gazing out, with her back to the room. She turned as Constance came in. The pale grey eyes that looked so vivid in her brown face rested on Constance with what she thought was hostility, but then the woman smiled and Constance realised that in a fine-boned, angular way she had remarkable beauty. She had taken off her raincoat, and it and her shoulder bag were lying on a chair. She was wearing a neat suit of a soft red with a deeper crimson blouse. She was holding a glass of sherry.

"Come in, Mrs. Lawley," Mrs. Barrow said. She was sitting in her usual place on the sofa beside the fireplace. "I'm afraid we've a lot of explaining to do, because we don't want you to think we're quite mad. Godfrey, give Mrs. Lawley some sherry, and come and sit here, dear." She patted the sofa beside her. "Oh dear, I don't really know where to begin."

"Begin with that slight slip-up of your daughter's," the woman by the window said as Constance sat down on the sofa beside Mrs. Barrow. "I hope I shan't embarrass you, Mrs. Lawley, but I can put it in quite a few words and that is how I prefer to do it. Colin is a son I had by mistake at a time when I had a job in Bracklington just fifteen years ago. But it happened that I didn't want to marry his father and I did want to marry an-

other man called Kenneth Pauling. He's an architect
and he'd just got a job with a big firm of building con-
tractors in Sydney. And he wanted to marry me, but not
plus a child. So when my parents offered to look after
the child, Ken and I quietly vanished away, and we all
thought it would be less upsetting for Colin to believe
we were dead than that we'd simply abandoned him.
We may have been wrong, and of course, he'd have had
to be told the truth sooner or later, as quite a lot of
people know I'm alive and one of them was sure to tell
him about it before he was much older. What none of
us knew, of course, was that he was going to turn out a
somewhat peculiar child, as I understand from my parents he has. I can see it's going to be difficult to get him
to take in what happened. Anyway, now you know the
facts."

"Would you like me to leave?" Constance asked.

She found something unnerving about the cool, hard
tone in which the woman had told her story. The faint
twang in her voice, Constance recognized, came from
what she had picked up of an Australian accent during
her years in Sydney.

Mrs. Barrow put her hand quickly on top of one of
Constance's.

"Leave? Why should you think we want you to
leave?"

"I only thought that with Mrs. Pauling here to look
after you, you might not need me any more," Constance replied.

"But do you want to go?" Mrs. Barrow asked. "Aren't
you comfortable here with us?"

"Of course I am," Constance said.

"Don't think of moving on my account," Margot
Pauling said. "I don't know what my plans are. If Colin

can't stand the sight of me, it might be best for me to move on soon. I may be moving anyway."

"Don't say that now that you're back here after all this time," Colonel Barrow said. "You must at least take some time to think out what you really want to do."

"You see, Mrs. Lawley, I haven't actually told you all the facts yet," the tall woman said. "That marriage of mine, for which I gave up Colin and one or two other things, such as a man who, I believe, was fairly genuinely in love with me, has come unstuck. I needn't go into why, but there were good reasons and I walked out on it a couple of days ago, and so here I am. But naturally I can't stay here indefinitely. I've got to earn a living and I can hardly do that in Long Meldon. I'll be moving on to London soon, I think."

"Darling, you know you can stay here as long as you like," Mrs. Barrow said. "Of course you won't stay for ever, but you can take your time and find yourself some really nice sort of job and just give us a little of the pleasure of your company after all this time."

Constance did not feel that the company of Margot Pauling would give her a great deal of pleasure, but her parents, of course, would feel differently about it.

"I'll get a room ready for Mrs. Pauling, shall I?" she said. "Which room shall it be?"

"The one on the top floor, if you'd be so very kind," Mrs. Barrow said. "The one next to Colin's. You know where the sheets and towels and everything are, don't you? Oh dear, I'm afraid this is more than you bargained for, but I do so hope you'll stay."

"You see, she doesn't trust me to look after things properly," Margot said, "so I also hope you'll stay."

Turning away, she gazed out into the garden again, perhaps looking for where Colin might be hiding or perhaps just looking at an English garden again after so long away from one.

Constance gulped her sherry and hurried out to the kitchen to inspect the roast in the oven.

She went to bed early that evening. Before she had served the dinner, she had heard Colin's voice in the drawing-room and wondered what he was making of the situation, but had restrained an inclination to eaves-drop. But when she was in bed, finding it very difficult to keep her attention on the detective story that she had brought with her, she found her thoughts straying with a sad sort of curiosity to the boy, faced, as he must feel himself to be, by a fantastic problem.

In the morning she took Mrs. Barrow's breakfast up to her in her bedroom, set the table in the dining-room for the colonel, his daughter, and his grandson, and then settled down at the kitchen table to drink her own coffee. She thought that if she could think of a good reason for it, she would like to go home. Until the evening before, she had been unusually happy in the household, very much preferring it to many others where she had worked, but the coming of Margot Pauling had already changed the atmosphere. Even if she made no difficulties of a practical nature, her mere presence seemed to have created a feeling that Constance was someone to be kept at arm's length. She had often encountered this in other households, but not after such a warm welcome as she had received here.

She had cleared the dining-table, made the beds, cleaned the bath, done a little dusting, and returned to the kitchen when Colin came into it. Though Constance had encountered Margot once or twice during the rudimentary housework that she had been doing, she had had no offers of help from her. All that Margot had said was that she hoped that she was not in the way; then she had strolled out on to the terrace where the table and the chessmen had been righted, had dropped into a chair, and had lighted a cigarette.

Seeing this, Constance had reflected that she must find something that could be used as an ashtray, because there was no such thing in any of the Barrows' rooms. She was looking at the china and glass in a cupboard in the kitchen for some dish or bowl that would do when Colin came in.

He stood watching her for a moment without saying anything and then asked, "What are you doing?"

"Looking for an ashtray," she answered. "Look, what do you think of this?" She held out a pretty little Davenport dish that she had just found in the cupboard.

"Why d'you want an ashtray?" he asked. "No one here smokes."

"Your mother does. She's almost a chain-smoker."

"I wish you wouldn't call her my mother," he said. "My mother's dead."

She gave him an uncertain look, wondering what he really thought.

"She isn't *my* mother," he said as if he were explaining something very simple which she should have understood without needing the explanation.

"The mother you've always dreamed of?" she asked. "She isn't like that?"

He sat down at the table, put his elbows on it, and took his head in his hands.

"Do you like me?" he asked abruptly.

She was taken aback by it, but answered calmly, "Of course I do."

"Don't say that!" he responded in a soft, violent tone. "Everyone says 'of course' this and 'of course' that and it doesn't mean anything. Everyone pretends to like me and says 'of course' they do, but nobody does."

"Oh, you're wrong, Colin," she said. "Think how your grandparents love you."

He gave a mocking little smile which reminded her suddenly of his mother.

"They've lied and lied to me," he said. "All my life they've lied to me. Do you lie to someone you love?"

She felt very helpless. "Sometimes more, I think, than to anyone else."

"No, you don't. If you do, it's because you don't trust them. That's just as bad as not loving them. Nobody's ever trusted me."

She supposed that in a sense he was right, but she said, "Of course they have."

"Of course, of course!" He brought his hands down with a bang on the table. "I wish you'd be serious. I thought you would be. You know what it's like here, you know I'm not wanted. This woman you call my mother didn't want me, and Grandma and Grandpa only look after me because if they didn't, people would talk. You don't know how often I've thought of running away."

"Where would you go to if you did?"

"How do I know? That would be the whole point of it—not knowing where I was going."

"What would you do for money?"

"Get odd jobs."

"Now it's you who aren't being serious," Constance said, but she was careful to keep her tone quiet to match his, as if they were having a reasonable discussion. "It isn't as easy as all that to get odd jobs."

"I'd manage. Or there are other things I could do. I've often thought about it, and now that this woman's come here, I'll have to do something."

"What kind of thing?"

He gave her an odd look that was almost sly.

"Oh, I'll think of something."

"Colin dear, you know that sooner or later you'll have to face the fact that she really is your mother." She did not know if this was the right sort of thing to say to him or if it would be wiser to keep silent. "She has her own difficulties, you know, and when she left you with your grandparents she really thought she was doing the best she could for you."

"Do you love your own children?" he asked.

Again she was taken by surprise. "Very much." But as she said it, she suddenly wondered how true it was that she still loved Irene and thought that it was strange that she had never asked herself this question before.

"Do you love them so much you'd die for them?" Colin asked. His tone was still quiet, yet there was extreme intensity in it and his eyes were blazing in his beautiful face. "Do you?"

"I suppose it would depend on the circumstances," she said, hoping that she did not betray how disturbing she found the question.

"Nobody's ever loved me enough for that," he said.

"Do you want someone to die for you then? I don't think it's a very nice thing to want."

"You might like to know if they'd do it, if you'd never been loved yourself."

"But you have been. I told you, your grandparents love you very much indeed."

He gave a little shake of his head. "And I told you, they've lied to me all my life. As they'd have gone on lying if that woman hadn't come here. And even now they're lying to me about my father. They won't talk about him. They won't tell me anything about him. And my mother says he was killed in a car crash and that the only lie I've been told is that she was with him.

She said it was because he was dead that she married another man and went to Australia. That's so silly."

Constance was inclined to think that it was very silly, but that the real silliness for which the old people and their daughter were sure to pay now was that the boy had not known the truth from the beginning. All the same, she wondered if the Barrows knew who his father was and what had happened to him. In Margot's very frank statement to Constance the evening before, it was the one thing that she had not mentioned.

Colin sat in silence for a moment; then, with the suddenness of most of his movements, he got up and left the kitchen. Constance sat down at the table, put her elbows on it, and took her head in her hands, just as Colin had. She felt that she had hopelessly mishandled the interview that she had had with the boy, yet did not know what line she might have taken with him that would have saved him from some of the intense unhappiness that he was experiencing now. And brooding about it did not help. After a little while she turned her attention to what she would give the family for lunch.

The simplest thing would be to give them some cold lamb left over from the evening before and some salad and then biscuits and cheese. But she had the evening to think about, and that meant that she must go shopping in the afternoon. She could go to the butcher to whom Colonel Barrow had introduced her the day before; alternatively she might drive into Bracklington and go to the shops she was used to and, while she was at it, pick up something as a birthday present for Colin.

This was what in the end she decided to do. When she had eaten her own lunch in the kitchen and cleared the table in the dining-room and Mrs. Barrow had gone upstairs for her afternoon rest, Constance told Colonel Barrow what she was going to do and that she would

not be away for very long, and then got her Mini out of
the garage and drove off. To be by herself without the
pressure of other people's problems felt very peaceful.
The day was sunny and warm, and she enjoyed the
drive to her home, where she had thought that she
might drop in for a few minutes to see that all was well
and if there were any letters for her.

Meanwhile, she had to decide what to buy for Colin.
It would have been so much easier if he had been a girl.
She could have bought her a pretty scarf or some little
trinket. And if he had been a few years younger, she
could have bought him a toy, and if he had been a little
older, perhaps a book. But a boy of fifteen of whom she
really knew very little was a problem. There must be
books that would interest him, but she did not know
what they were. In the end, feeling that it was a confes-
sion of failure, she decided on a book token. Perhaps it
would give him pleasure to go and choose something for
himself. Stopping at a bookshop near her home, she
went in and bought the token, and then drove on to her
house.

There was no mail except an electricity bill and an
envelope asking for Christian Aid. Putting them on her
writing-table so that she would not forget to deal with
them when she came back to stay, she went quickly
round the house and saw that all was well. There had
been no break-in, no tank had overflowed. It was a
small house in a Victorian terrace, with only four rooms
but all of them lofty and of reasonable size. She had
moved into it after her husband's death, when Peter and
Irene had both left home and the house where she had
lived for twenty-five years had started to feel depress-
ingly big and empty. She stayed in the little house now
for about ten minutes and was about to leave when

something stopped her. Going to her writing-table, she sat down at it and began to write a letter to Irene.

It was a thing that she very seldom did. She did not believe that letters from her were particularly welcome. But something about the talk that she had had with Colin made her feel that if her daughter should want to be free of her, it should not be because of any rejection by her. It was a short letter, telling Irene where she was working and a little about the problems that seemed to be developing there, saying it would be nice to see her sometime and asking her if she was happy and well. Leaving the house, she dropped the letter into a post-box near it, then went on to the supermarket where she did most of her shopping, bought some veal escalopes and some fillet steaks, some fruit and some vegetables, and set off for Long Meldon.

She arrived at Riverside in time to take tea into the drawing-room and found Margot Pauling sitting there by herself. She was wearing blue slacks and a blue-and-white-striped shirt and would have looked coolly handsome if there had not been something ravaged about her face, healthy though it looked, tanned by the Australian sun. She seemed to make an effort to be courteous to Constance.

"Isn't it strange, I feel far more exhausted today than I did yesterday?" she said. "It's trying to get used to the difference in time, I suppose. You're about ten hours behind us. And the journey itself took about twenty-five hours and I can never sleep on an aeroplane. I know I could have broken the journey at Singapore, but once I'd made up my mind to come home, I wanted to get here as fast as possible. When I'm feeling a bit more normal, I'll give you some help."

"It's all right; I can manage," Constance said. "It's my job, after all."

"I've got to look for a job," Margot said. "I've been running an interior decorator's in Sydney, and perhaps I could get into something of the same sort here, but I dare say there aren't so many opportunities going. I trained as a nurse once, years ago, but I'd be hopelessly out of date now. And I was never meant for that sort of work anyhow. Sick people— Well, of course I know what's the matter with me: I'm thoroughly selfish. Sick people rather bore me, that's the truth."

Constance could not resist saying, "And children too?"

Margot gave a cold little smile. "You're thinking of Colin? That child hates me, can't you see that? He doesn't want me to take him over. And anyway, how would I look after him if I was working? He's much better off with Ma and Pa than he would be with me."

"You may be right." It was Constance's formula for the times when she did not want to be drawn into an argument.

"Certainly I'm right," Margot said with a curious bitterness in her voice, as if after all she was hurt by her own conclusion. Yet probably she was right, Constance thought and, feeling a little guiltily glad that the problem of the boy and his future was not one to which she had to find a solution, went out to the kitchen and to the cup of tea that she had left there for herself.

At about six o'clock Colonel Barrow, as was his custom, came out to the kitchen to invite her to join the family in the drawing-room for sherry. She explained that what she was cooking for dinner would need her attention, but he persuaded her to go with him for a very quick drink. Mrs. Barrow had come downstairs, and she and Margot were sitting side by side on the sofa, Margot with a cigarette in her mouth, while Colin was on the terrace, poring over his chessboard. He

glanced up as Constance came into the drawing-room,
but his attention immediately returned with a look of
deep absorption to his game against himself. It was only
when Conrad Greer suddenly appeared on the terrace
that he started up and exclaimed, "Conrad! I say, that's
super. Come and have a game."

Sweeping all the chessmen over, he started setting
them up for the beginning of a new game.

Greer said, "All right, just one, in a moment."

Then he came into the drawing-room to greet the Barrows and saw Margot.

He went rigid, staying where he was just inside the
French window as if he could not move. But it was only
for an instant. Then he came forward, smiling, and said,
"Well, well, Margot. What a surprise."

She gave him one of her tight-lipped little smiles.

"You've a good memory for faces, Conrad," she said.

"You haven't changed at all."

"Oh, I've changed."

"It doesn't show."

"Because you've changed yourself," she said. "But
one doesn't live as I've had to live without having it
written on one's face, line by line."

"Yes, the lines are there, I won't pretend they aren't,
but they spell out much the same message as ever."

"Conrad!" Colin was calling from the terrace. "Conrad, come and play a game!"

Greer did not answer.

"Well, aren't you going to play with the boy?"
Margot asked.

"Not just now," he answered. "Another time."

"Conrad!" Colin cried. "You said you would."

"Yes, but I've just remembered something else I've
got to do. I really haven't time to stay. I'm sorry,
Colin."

He stepped out on to the terrace and stood for a moment looking down at the boy, but it was as if he did not see him. Then he walked quickly away through the garden.

Constance wondered how it could have been that until that moment when the man and the boy had gazed at one another across the chessboard, she had never noticed what a remarkable resemblance there was between them.

She finished her drink and went out to the kitchen. She decided to cook the veal that she had bought in Bracklington. As she went to work preparing it, she wondered if the Barrows knew that Conrad Greer was Colin's father. Once having seen the resemblance, it seemed to her impossible that they did not. But thinking over the brief scene in the drawing-room, it seemed to her possible that they had never done so. They had shown no embarrassment when he had appeared, no evidence that they knew of any relationship between him and their daughter. The likeness between the boy and the man might have been something that had developed slowly and to which they were so accustomed that they had never noticed it.

Margot helped Constance that evening to clear the dining-table and stack the dishwasher, and when this was done and Constance was thinking of leaving the kitchen and going up to her bedroom, Margot lingered, looking at Constance with an interest that she had not yet shown.

Constance was feeling unusually tired. It was possible, she thought, that she would soon have to give up the kind of work that she was doing and look for something less demanding. Meanwhile, she wished that Margot would go, but lighting a cigarette and sitting

down at the table, Margot showed no inclination to do
so.

"You live in Bracklington, don't you?" she said.

"Yes," Constance answered.

"Why?"

The question seemed an odd one to Constance.
"Well, why not?" she said.

"But something must have brought you here in the
first place, or were you born here?"

"No, I was born in London," Constance said. "But
my husband was a lecturer in the Polytechnic here for
twenty years."

"And you never wanted to get away?"

"Why should I?"

"I'd have thought, if you've no ties, you might have
looked for somewhere more interesting."

"Nearly all my friends live here, and at my age you
don't make new friends easily."

"Oh, you've friends here?"

"Well, naturally."

"Is Conrad Greer a friend of yours?"

Constance understood now to where the conversation
had been steered.

"I believe I've met him about three times," she said.
"I don't think that amounts to friendship."

"No." Margot seemed to think this over carefully and
then repeated, "No. But you know if he still runs that
antique shop, I expect."

"Yes, I even bought something from him once."

"And that woman Julie What's-her-name, does she
still work for him?"

"I believe so."

"Don't you know her?"

"No. I've met her sister, who runs a café in Long
Meldon, but I've never met Julie."

"I used to think they'd marry, you know. I wonder why they haven't."

It might be, Constance thought, that Margot herself was the reason. Alternatively, it might be that Colin was the problem. If Greer had acquired a wife and a home where between them they could have looked after the boy, Greer might have assumed that they should claim him, and that perhaps might not have suited Julie. People can become as addicted to antiques as artists to painting, as composers to music, and giving up her work in the shop to look after a child who, so Constance had been told by Colonel Barrow, did not even like her might not have appealed to her at all. Perhaps Colin had been right when he had said that no one had ever wanted him.

"Your parents know Mr. Greer very well, I believe," she said.

"They say he's always been very good to Colin," Margot remarked.

"I believe he has."

"Though Colin's not exactly a normal boy, is he? It may sound an absurd thing to say, but he rather frightens me. Those great eyes of his—"

She broke off as the front doorbell rang.

Constance was about to go to answer it when she heard the footsteps of the colonel crossing the hall, so she pulled a chair out from the table and sat down, wishing that Margot would go, but the young woman did not move. Margot only became curiously tense as she listened to her father's voice and that of the visitor, and drawing smoke deeply into her lungs, she breathed it out again slowly through her nostrils. With astonishment Constance saw that the hand with which she held her cigarette was shaking.

The kitchen door opened.

"Margot," Colonel Barrow said, "it's your husband."

She moved swiftly then, snatching at the handle of the back door, wrenching it open, and disappearing into the garden.

Colonel Barrow came into the kitchen, followed by a tall man who looked about the same age as Margot, though his hair was already grey. He had a square face with strong, stubborn-looking features, a wide mouth, and light brown eyes spaced far apart under thick brown eyebrows. He was wearing grey slacks and a light quilted jacket and was carrying a small suitcase.

"That," he observed, looking at the door that Margot had left open behind her, "would seem to be that."

Like her, he had picked up a faint trace of Australian in his accent.

"Mrs. Lawley, this is our son-in-law, Kenneth Pauling," Colonel Barrow said. "I'm afraid we can't put you up here, Ken; all our spare rooms are occupied, but there's a very pleasant pub in the village that lets rooms. I'll ring them up and make sure they've got one free. Meanwhile, come and meet Dorothea and have a drink."

"Good evening, Mrs. Lawley," the stranger said. "Perhaps I'd better go straight to the pub, Colonel. I wouldn't want to keep my wife out in your garden all the evening."

"That's nonsense," Colonel Barrow said. "Seeing you suddenly like that, when she never dreamt you'd follow her, gave her a shock, that's all."

"And what does she think I'm going to do to her now that I'm here?" Kenneth Pauling asked. "Strangle the idiot woman?"

"I think it's just that this breakup of your marriage and coming back to England and all that sort of thing has upset her more than you'd think," Colonel Barrow said. "Her mother and I have both noticed that she's very nervous."

"Who said that our marriage has broken up?" Kenneth Pauling asked.

"Well, she did."

"I suppose she would. But we've a bit of talking to do before it's settled. You can't just pack a bag and write a note and prop it against a whisky bottle and get on a plane and think that's written off a dozen years of living together without a word of discussion."

"Is that what she did?"

"Just about."

"Anyway, she'll come in presently. So come and see Dorothea and have a drink and . . . and, of course, meet Colin."

"Colin? That's the boy, isn't it? But I think, if you don't mind, Colonel, I'll go to that pub straight away, then come back tomorrow when Margot's got more used to the idea that I'm around. But, of course, I'd like to see Mrs. Barrow first."

"I'll ring up the Green Dragon at once," Colonel Barrow said. "I'm sure they'll have a room for you, but it's as well to be sure. Then I'll drive you down."

"It's all right, I can walk," Pauling said, "if you'll tell me where the place is."

"I could drive Mr. Pauling to the Green Dragon," Constance said, "if you don't mind dinner being a little late."

"Ah, that would be splendid, if you really don't mind." The colonel, she thought, would be glad to be free of his son-in-law and have a chance to discuss the situation as soon as possible with his daughter. "Dorothea's been ill, you know, Ken. She's only just out of hospital. And Mrs. Lawley's come here to help us. Now come along and I'll phone the pub."

He led the man out of the kitchen.

It was not long before he returned and Constance took him out to the garage, drove her Mini out of it, and waited for him to get into it. As he settled in the seat beside her, she said, "They'd a room for you all right at the Green Dragon, had they?"

"Luckily, yes," he said. "I'm not welcome here, am I? I didn't really think about that when I started off. I didn't know about Mrs. Barrow having been ill, and I didn't think Margot would run for her life when she saw me. It looks as if I've taken a long journey for nothing. Forgive me, but could you tell me who you are?"

Constance drove out into the lane.

"I'm housekeeper here for a week," she said, "till Mrs. Barrow gets a bit better. I take on this kind of job from time to time."

"They aren't specially friends of yours then?" he asked.

"I never met them until Wednesday when I started work here."

"So you didn't know Margot in the old days? I mean, before she came with me to Australia."

"No."

"I suppose they always thought I was wrong, leaving the boy on their hands."

"Perhaps. I don't know. They're very fond of him."

"What was really wrong with the idea I had then was that she and I could make a success of marriage after what had happened. Anyway, that's how it looks now. It isn't the first time she's left me, you know."

"But it's the first time she's come all the way home, isn't it?"

"Yes."

"And she always came back to you before?"

"When I fetched her back."

"Perhaps she'll go back to you now if you really want her back."

"Oh, I want her. Damn the bloody woman, I've always loved her, though she's as neurotic as hell. Tell me, what's the boy like?"

Constance took so long to reply that after a little he said, "Something wrong with him, is there?"

"I don't know quite what to say," she answered. "He isn't exactly normal."

"You're saying he's crazy, are you?"

"Oh no, just that he's sort of strange. I think he's really quite a clever boy."

"I get it," he said. "All my fault because of taking his mother away from him. That's what the psychiatrists say, isn't it? But that was her idea as much as mine, you know. I didn't care much one way or the other. Look, I don't know why I'm talking to you like this. I don't want to trouble you with my problems."

"It's an odd thing, but doing the job I do I find people often want to unload their problems on me." She was driving the car across the bridge into the main street of the village. "I suppose it's because they're usually ill or under a strain of some sort, and it's often easier to talk to a stranger than to someone you know well."

"So I've been told, though I can't say I've ever experienced it before. Well, what about coming into the Green Dragon with me and having a drink? Perhaps you've some problems of your own you'd like to unload. I'm not as bad as you might think at listening."

She thought that he might be very good at listening. In spite of his looking big and tough, there was a warmth and gentleness in his manner that made her wonder why Margot had left him. Infidelities perhaps? A tendency to become quickly and easily involved with other women?

She answered, "I'd like to, but I've got to get back now to get that dinner cooked as soon as possible." She drew up at the entrance to the Green Dragon, which had once been a simple village pub but was now a quite sophisticated little hotel. It was a lopsided-looking building that had been painted a pale green and had a slate roof that sagged in a wavy line against the sky. "I understand you'll be coming up to Riverside tomorrow."

"D'you know, I'm not sure of that," he said as he got out of the car. "I'll think about it. Thanks for the drive."

As he spoke, Constance saw another man walk up to the entrance to the pub and, catching sight of Pauling, suddenly pause.

It was Conrad Greer.

For a moment the two of them stood looking at one another in startled rigidity and then, with an air of cautious formality, shook hands.

Constance decided that it was time for her to drive away, and turning back, she drove back the way that she had come. She had no sooner put the Mini back in the garage and gone into the kitchen by the back door, which as usual was unlocked, than Colin came running out to meet her.

"Where is he, what have you done with him?" he cried, catching hold of her by the arms and starting to shake her. "That's the man who stole my mother, isn't it? He's why everybody's always lied to me. All my life, nothing but lies. I'm going to kill him. I'm going to kill everybody. That's what I'll do."

Giving an eerie wail, he turned and dashed for the staircase up to his room.

Four

Colin appeared to have recovered somewhat by the time
Constance announced to the family that dinner was
ready, for though she did not see him again that evening, she found, when she cleared the table, that someone had sat and eaten at his place. Colonel Barrow and
Margot had cleared the table between the courses, so
Constance had not had to go into the dining-room until
the meal was over, and Colin had disappeared by then.
When she took coffee into the drawing-room, he was
not there. She went upstairs as soon as she could, got
into bed, and resumed reading her detective story.

But she soon laid it down as she tried to think how
she would feed the family over the weekend. She would
have to go shopping again in the morning. This was
unlike her. Usually when she took on a job of the kind
that she was doing here, she immediately planned everything in advance, reduced shopping trips to a mini-

mum, knew exactly what she would cook next day, and felt that she had everything under control. But here things did not feel under control.

She felt that anything might happen to upset any planning that she might do. The front door bell might ring again, and heaven knows who might appear then. The two men whom she had left together at the Green Dragon perhaps, arriving together to make some fantastic scene about the woman whom they had once shared or the child who belonged to neither of them. What kind of scene it might be she could not imagine, any more than she could guess what had happened after she had driven away from the pub. Perhaps it had all been very friendly. Perhaps they had even been glad to meet again after all these years. But if that doorbell rang again, she was not going to answer it. She had come here as a housekeeper, not as a marriage counsellor. And she was very tired.

After a little while she laid her book aside, turned out the light, and soon fell asleep.

Next morning, when she had cleared away the breakfast, she sat down at the kitchen table to make out a shopping list. As next day was Sunday, some sirloin, she thought, would be appropriate. And that meant that the day after, the family could eat cold beef. Then perhaps a gooseberry pie with cream might follow the sirloin. The list grew long as she thought of all the things which it might be useful to buy, but at last, at about half past ten, she got into the Mini and set off for the village.

It was as she was coming out of the butcher's that she met Kenneth Pauling. He had been buying a newspaper at the grocer's. He greeted Constance pleasantly.

"You wouldn't have a drink with me yesterday evening," he said, "but what about some coffee now? I'm told they give you a very good cup of coffee at this place called Jenny's."

"I haven't got long," Constance said. "I've a busy morning ahead of me."

"But you'll come—good." He took the basket that she held and carried it for her towards Jenny's Café. "How do you like it at the Barrows'?"

She did not answer at once because just then a car came out from the garage beside the café and she saw that Jennifer Hyland was driving it. Jennifer saw her and smiled and waved, and then drove off down the village street towards the bridge.

"You asked me something," Constance said. "Oh yes, how do I like it at the Barrows'? Very much on the whole."

They went into the café together.

"Not altogether then?" he said as they sat down at a table in the curved bay window.

"That would be rather much to hope for, wouldn't it?" Looking at his strong, square face it struck Constance that he looked as if he had not slept much. There were shadows under his light brown eyes and deeper lines about his mouth than she remembered seeing there before. "When I take these jobs, I don't take for granted they're going to be easy."

"What's difficult here?" he asked.

"A tendency unexpected strangers have of turning up," she said. "The emotional atmosphere is getting rather highly charged."

"In other words, you're telling me I shouldn't have come."

"Oh no, I'm not telling you anything, though you want me to, don't you? Why don't you just ask me what you want to know?"

They had given their order for coffee to a tall slim

woman who, it seemed to Constance, she had met before. Yet she did not think that she could have done so.
Where could they have met? The woman was in her
late thirties, with fair hair drawn straight back from a
somewhat stern-looking, handsome face and a casual air
of waiting on them as if they were of no account to her.
It was as she walked away that Constance suddenly realised why she felt that there was something familiar
about her. In spite of being tall and slender instead of
short and stocky and having sleek straight hair instead
of a mop of curls, she had a distinct resemblance to
Jennifer, whom Constance had just seen leaving the
café. So this must be her sister, Julie, who no doubt was
helping out in the café because on Saturday the antique
shop in Bracklington was closed. And if Constance was
right that this was Julie Hyland, she had certainly met
her briefly before. She had been in the background in
the shop when Constance had gone in to buy her Chelsea bowl.

Spooning sugar into his coffee, Pauling said, "I'd like
to know how long Margot stayed out in the garden last
night."

"I don't know," Constance answered. "She'd come in
by the time I got back."

"Because she knew I wasn't there any longer."

"I suppose so."

"Has she ever talked about me?"

"Not to me. She told me that Colin wasn't your child
and that you'd only marry her if she left him behind
when you went off to Australia. But yesterday evening
you told me that was her idea as much as yours."

He nodded, but his gaze had become abstracted.

"I did that, did I?" he said. "Perhaps it's true. I always wanted to think so. I didn't like the feeling of
having ditched the kid. I wanted her to be at least as

responsible as I was. But it may have been one of the things that have always been wrong between us. Perhaps she was hankering after him."

"I haven't seen any sign of that in her since she got here. She hasn't made any effort to get on good terms with him. To be honest, I don't think she likes him."

"Is that because he isn't quite normal?"

"How do you know about that? Oh, of course, I told you that myself, didn't I? And you've been talking to Mr. Greer."

"Who's Colin's father. You know that, don't you?"

"I guessed it."

"The way things happened, I ought to have realised then that it would be useless for Margot and me to go ahead with our marriage. We were engaged, you know, and I had to go away to work on a job in Scotland, and when I got home from it, she was pregnant. And that's how it's gone on, except that she's been more careful that there shouldn't be any more Colins. She didn't want us to have a child. I wasn't keen on the idea myself, so that didn't matter, but the devil of it is, I'm fairly violent by nature and I've beaten her up more than once. Somehow we've always managed to forgive one another, but this last time we both went rather far and I think she got frightened. I know I did. I hadn't realised before just how much of the brute there is stored up in me. It's not a nice discovery. And when she ran out on me, all I could think of was that I'd got to follow her and persuade her that it would never happen again and get her to come back. But you saw how she bolted the moment she saw me."

"You called her an idiot woman then, as if it were absurd for her to be afraid of you," Constance said. "But that isn't quite what you're saying now. Perhaps it wasn't absurd."

He sighed. "No, I'm very mixed up. I was embarrassed yesterday evening because you and the old man were there to see what happened when Margot and I met. And I think, until that did happen, I hadn't taken the situation as seriously as I should. Perhaps what I was really thinking of was what an idiot she'd been to think she could go on getting away with her infidelities without pushing me beyond what I could take. I had an idea that if I followed her here, it might be enough of a shock for her to make her realise we'd got to do a lot of talking before we called everything off and that perhaps both of us could change and make a reasonable success of things after all."

"What I really don't understand," Constance said, "is why you're telling me all this. What is it you really want from me?"

"A spot of sympathy perhaps."

She shook her head. "I think there's more to it than that."

"All right then, I've been wondering if you could persuade her to come and talk to me here. I don't want to go back to the house. I'm not exactly welcome there, would you say? I think Margot may have given the old people a version of what's gone on between us which has rather suppressed the provocation I've had. And to tell you the truth, I don't want to run into that boy. He can't much want to meet me either."

"I'm sure you're right there."

"Well, will you ask Margot to come and meet me in the Green Dragon?"

"Yes, I can do that. And if she doesn't come, I promise it won't be because I haven't delivered your message."

"I understand that. You might add, when you give it

to her, that in the bar of the Green Dragon nothing very dangerous to her can happen."

"What puzzles me," she said, "is why you want to stick together. I couldn't endure a relationship of the kind you've described."

He gave a tight little grin. "It rather puzzles me myself, but there it is."

"You don't really think you're going to get anywhere with her, do you?"

He did not answer, but finished his coffee. Constance had already finished hers. The brisk little woman in the pink overall whom Constance had seen when she and Colonel Barrow had come into the café with Jennifer came to their table and tried to persuade them to have another cup. When they both refused, she presented the bill.

"Where are you going now?" Pauling asked as he and Constance went out into the street.

"I've some more shopping to do," she said, "then I must get back to Riverside and get on with my job."

"And you'll give Margot that message of mine as soon as you can?"

"Yes," she assured him.

As if it had only just occurred to him to answer her last question, he said, "Of course it won't do any good, but we've got to talk things over. Money, for instance. Our home in Sydney—what's going to happen to it? Do we go ahead with a divorce? We've got to talk. She can have money if she wants it. Tell her that, though it may not help to persuade her to come. Goodbye for now. Thanks for listening to me."

He turned towards the Green Dragon while Constance crossed the street to the grocer's.

She spent longer than she had intended in the shop. Her nerves were on edge after the talk in the café. She could not decide whether she liked or disliked Kenneth Pauling and whether she was sorry for him or thought him dreadful. Thinking of her own marriage, which had been tender and faithful, marred only by the briefest of quarrels, yet which had had passion in it too, she told herself that however long she lived, she would never understand other people. She wandered slowly round the shop, filling the wire basket provided for the purpose from the shelves with far more things than were on the list that she had made before setting out, and she found this soothing. After a while she began to feel that there was even a rather gruesome kind of comedy in the situation in which she found herself.

She had come to Long Meldon to act as housekeeper to an elderly couple, retired army people, kindly, conventional, considerate, the only strangeness in the household at first being their somewhat maladjusted grandson. They loved him, however, and he appeared in his way a sufficiently likeable boy. But then there had appeared on the scene a distinctly maladjusted daughter, followed by a maladjusted husband, while in the background there lurked the daughter's abandoned lover, father of the child and devoted to him. And these people were showing signs of turning to Constance for help. To Constance, who had had so few problems in her life. It really was rather funny.

It was true that she had had her problems with Irene. Those at times had seemed of immense importance to her. Other people, she had thought, did not have such peculiar daughters, and it had bewildered her that two such normal people as she believed her husband and herself to have been should have produced such a freak. But in Long Meldon, it seemed, freaks were thick on the ground, and it was just her fate that she was stuck in the midst of them. Until next Wednesday. That was really not so far away. She could put up with it some-how. Heading for her car with all her purchases, she got into it and started the drive back to Riverside.

Driving the car into the garage, she entered the house by the back door, which as usual was unlocked. She saw at once that Jennifer Hyland had been here before her, for in the middle of the kitchen table there was a large birthday cake. It was a very fine cake covered with white icing with elaborate pink decorations and with the words "Many happy returns, Colin" inscribed on its top.

Constance stood looking at the cake, considering it. It could not stay where it was, because she would soon be needing the table to work at, and besides, there was the question of whether or not Colin was to see the cake before his birthday tomorrow or whether it was to be kept a secret. She decided to ask Mrs. Barrow, and put-ting down the full basket that she had brought with her into the kitchen, she went to the drawing-room.

She started to scream.

She screamed and screamed.

It was a moment before she realised that it was she herself who was screaming. She heard the sound of it and she felt a constriction in her throat, but some time passed—she never remembered how long—before she connected the two things. When that happened, she became abruptly silent and, stumbling out of the room, went to the telephone in the hall. She dialled 999.

"Police," she said. "Please, at once . . . My name? Oh, it's Lawley . . . The address? Riverside, Long Mel-don . . . I've just found four bodies in a room here . . . Yes, *four* . . . Yes, I said *four,* and I want the po-lice at once."

She seemed to have to wait for a never-ending time, yet at the same time, she knew that it was almost at once that a man's voice said, "Police. Bracklington. Yes?"

"Please send someone here at once," she said. "Riverside, Long Meldon. I've only just got in and I found . . ." She began to feel that she might be sick before she could say any more, but she forced herself to control it. "I found four people all dead in the drawing-room . . . Do I know who they are? Yes, they're Colonel and Mrs. Barrow and their daughter, Mrs. Pauling, and her son. I think they've all been shot. There's a pistol or a revolver or something like that lying on the floor . . . Yes, I'm quite sure they're all dead . . . No, I don't know when it happened, I've been out, I told you, and only just got in . . . I work here, that's why I found them. Please send someone at once."

She was told that someone would be with her almost immediately. She put the telephone down and only then realised that she felt deathly cold all over. The cold seemed to have got into her bones and to be spreading from them through the rest of her body, so that she shivered violently. There was a moment when the scene before her went completely black; then a light that was almost too lurid came back and she saw that she was standing with her hand still on the telephone and that the door into the room where she had seen unspeakable things was open. She shot into the kitchen and slammed the door shut behind her. She felt as if she were in some extreme kind of danger which came seeping towards her through the closed door from that other room and that it was going to engulf her and smother her.

Then she began to come to herself and sat down in a chair at the table, still feeling the chill in her blood, but recognizing it with the beginning of rationality as a symptom of shock and understanding that she could look at the door without seeing something terrible come through it. She was not in any danger unless it happened that a murderer was loose in the house and was going to come looking for her. But the murderer was in that room, as dead as his victims.

Her eyes suddenly fell on the birthday cake on the table before her. "Many happy returns, Colin." She felt tears gathering in her eyes and beginning to spill on to her cheeks. Folding her arms on the table, she hid her face in them so that she need not go on looking at the cake.

When the police came, she went to meet them at the front door with a rather creditable appearance of calm. A man of about forty, of medium height, with wide shoulders, an almost triangular face, wide at the temples, sharp at the chin, a high forehead from which the brown hair had begun to recede, and small, shrewd, bright blue eyes, introduced himself as Detective Inspector Frayne.

She said, "Come in." Then she stood back and gestured at the door of the drawing-room. "In there."

She watched him as he went to the door, followed by a tall, powerful-looking young man who stood just behind him, looking over his shoulder into the room.

This man said, "Christ!" then clapped a hand over his mouth as if, like her, he felt an impulse to be sick. But it seemed to be only momentary, for he seemed collected enough as he followed the inspector into the room.

Constance wished that they would close the door, but realised that they were following the regulations concerning touching nothing. After a moment they both emerged from the room.

The inspector said to her, "Have you got any brandy?"

"I don't know," she said. "Perhaps. Do you want some?"

"No, but you do," he said. "Where do they keep it?"

"In the dining-room, I suppose. I don't know." She pointed. "In there."

He took her by the arm and guided her into the dining-room and to a chair at the long mahogany table. Going to the tall old sideboard, he started opening its cupboards till he found what he was looking for, a bottle of brandy and some glasses. As she watched him doing it, Constance had a feeling that she had seen something like this happen before; then she realised that what he reminded her of as he seemed to make himself strangely at home in the house was of how she herself behaved when she went to take up a new post. She always had to learn where her employers kept their china and their cooking-pots, their sheets and towels, as well as what food they had in their refrigerator or freezer. She always had to go searching through the house, opening cupboard doors and drawers until she knew where she could put her hand on anything she wanted. She had never thought that a policeman might be in the habit of doing virtually the same.

Pouring out some brandy for her, he said, "I'll be with you in a minute," and went out.

She heard him speaking on the telephone in the hall. She supposed that he was giving instructions to someone in Bracklington. Soon, no doubt, more men would arrive with cameras and with chalk to outline where the bodies lay and with equipment for the search for fingerprints, and a doctor, of course. And after all that, no doubt, the press. The press! She shuddered. Would she be able to avoid the press or would she have to talk to them? As soon as news of what had happened in the house got out, they would be certain to descend on it. Massacres do not go unreported.

She swallowed some brandy and felt it conflict with her inward chill and quickly drank some more. It seemed to steady her, and with a sigh as if of deep emotional exhaustion, she closed her eyes.

But as soon as she did that, she saw again what she had seen in the room. Mrs. Barrow had been sitting on the sofa by the fireplace and Colonel Barrow had been sitting beside her. Margot Pauling had been in a heap on the floor, just inside the French window. Colin had been lying on his back in the middle of the room. And they had all had blood on them. A terrible lot of blood which looked very red and wet, as if it had only just started to flow. Mrs. Barrow's face was half-hidden in a stream of it that seemed to come from a hole in her forehead. The colonel had a great blotch of blood covering his chest. Margot's wounds could not be seen because of the way that she had collapsed, covering them, but there was a mess of blood on the carpet near her head. And half of Colin's head seemed to have been blasted away. There had been a revolver close to his right hand.

Constance opened her eyes again as she heard the detective inspector come back into the room. The big man with him was introduced to her as Detective Sergeant Randall. She could hear that there was someone else in the house and was told by the inspector that there was a constable out there, keeping an eye on things.

"If you're up to it," he went on, "there are a few things I'd like to ask you before the others get here. It'll save time later."

"Go ahead," she said.

"Well, first, who are you?"

She told him her name and her home address and explained what her position was in the house. The sergeant had taken a notebook out of a pocket and began to write in it.

"And this morning you went out?" the inspector asked.

"Yes."

"Why did you do that?"

"To do some shopping. When I'm on a job like this, I take over everything—shopping, cooking, and so on. There's a Mrs. Newcome who comes in twice a week here to do the basic cleaning, but I do everything else."

"What time did you set out?"

"I think it was about half past ten."

"And was everything normal then?"

"Normal? Yes— No— I suppose so. I don't know. It can't have been, can it?"

"But did you notice anything unusual?"

"No, but I think that was my fault. I ought to have noticed something. If I'd taken the boy seriously last night . . . It was the boy who did it, wasn't it?"

"That's how it looks, but it's a bit too early to say anything for sure. It looks as if he somehow got hold of a gun and killed the other three and then himself. But we'd better not commit ourselves yet. What happened last night that you didn't take seriously?"

She sipped some brandy. "Perhaps I'd better explain about the household here; then you'll understand. Colonel and Mrs. Barrow have been living here for some years with their grandson, Colin. And Colin was brought up to believe that his parents had been killed in a car crash. But the truth is that he was the illegitimate son of their daughter, who . . . who's in that room. The one by the window," her voice cracked as she said it. "And she didn't want him and left him with her

parents and got married to a man called Pauling, who
was going out to a job in Australia, and she stayed there
without Colin knowing of her existence until last
Thursday, when she suddenly walked in here. She'd
broken up with her husband and come back to England,
saying she was going to stay and look for a job. And her
coming like that and his discovery that she'd been alive
all these years was a terrible shock for Colin. And he
wasn't altogether a normal boy at the best of times."

"What was wrong with him?"

"I don't know how to put it exactly. I don't know
much about that sort of thing. He wasn't exactly what
you'd call handicapped, but he was undeveloped in
some ways, yet clever in others, and very emotional,
and yet he didn't seem really able to care for anybody.
He was obsessed with the belief that nobody wanted
him."

"Didn't the old people want him? Weren't they good
to him?"

"They were very good to him."

"Then why did he have that idea?"

"I think it was just the kind of boy he was. And
when he discovered that his mother was alive and when
he came face to face with her, he became sort of wild
with fury that he'd been lied to all his life. And that
seemed to be very important to him, that he'd been told
so many lies."

"Can't say I blame him," the inspector observed. "I
get told a good many lies in the course of my work, and
it doesn't improve my temper. What about the man
Pauling? He's stayed in Australia, has he?"

"No, he followed his wife here. He's in Long Meldon."

The sergeant again muttered, "Christ!" Constance
began to wonder if it was his only word.

"He's staying at the Green Dragon in the village," she said. "He arrived here yesterday evening, hoping, as I understand it, to persuade his wife to go back with him. And Colin saw him and discovered who he was and shouted at me that he'd stolen his mother and that he was going to kill him and was going to kill everyone else too. Then he dashed up to his room, and I didn't see him again until . . . until just now. And I felt terribly sorry for him, but I never thought for a moment of taking him seriously. I mean, children so often make fearful threats, but they've forgotten them in a few minutes when they've calmed down. I didn't understand that Colin wasn't going to calm down. If I had, if I hadn't been so blind and ignorant about people like him, I ought to have been able to prevent this happening."

Inspector Frayne gave her a long, thoughtful look, as if he had not made up his mind as to whether she was at least partly to blame for what had happened or whether he should reassure her that she should not start blaming herself for what could not have been prevented by anyone.

"That gun," he said, "do you know anything about it?"

"No."

"It might have been Colonel Barrow's. A war souvenir. There are a lot more of those around than there ought to be. I wonder if he had a licence for it."

"I don't know. No one ever said anything about there being a gun in the house."

"But if there was one, the boy might have known about it, I suppose."

"Yes, I suppose so."

"And might have known how to fire it?"

"Well, he was clever at some things."

"We'll have to check up on it. Now you went into the village shopping at about half past ten. By car?"

"Yes."

"So it didn't take you long to get there. And when you came back you discovered that slaughter in the other room and you phoned 999 straight away. I've a note of that. That was at about a quarter to twelve. So you'd spent more than an hour shopping. You did a good deal, did you?"

"No, it wasn't like that." All at once she felt distrust of him, wondering what words he might be trying to put into her mouth, and why he might be doing it.

"What wasn't?" he asked.

"I met Mr. Pauling outside the grocer's, and he asked me to have coffee with him and we went into Jenny's Café—and that reminds me!" She stopped, startled at herself.

"Yes?"

"Colin's birthday cake! You see, it was his birthday tomorrow, and Jennifer Hyland was making a birthday cake for him. And as Mr. Pauling and I were going to the café, I saw her drive off and she waved to me. She was coming in this direction. And when I got back here, I came in by the back door because I knew it wouldn't be locked and I saw the birthday cake on the kitchen table. So she came here sometime during the morning. Whether it was before or after the shooting I don't know, but somehow it seems to me . . ." She paused.

"Yes?" he said again.

"I was just going to say, it seems to me it could have been after, because what I'd have expected her to do would have been to go to the front door and ring the bell and only if nobody answered it go round to the back and let herself in and leave the cake. And of course, if it was after the shooting, no one could have answered. But I'm only guessing. I think she knew the Barrows pretty well, and perhaps she knew she could get in at the back and left the cake there as a surprise for them."

"You said her name was—"

"Jennifer Hyland. She runs Jenny's Café."

"And you're sure she was here this morning?"

"She must have been."

"Because of the cake. I think I'd like to look at this cake."

Constance stood up and led the way to the kitchen. There was something dreadful to her about the cake with its cheerful message, "Many happy returns, Colin." But Inspector Frayne looked at it with considerable approval.

"Artistic job," he said. "A professional, this Miss Hyland?"

"Oh yes."

"And it's certain she came up to deliver it this morning?"

"Well, it wasn't there when I left and I saw her setting out from the café as Mr. Pauling and I went into it, so I suppose she must have come here."

"I think we'd better talk to her." He took hold of his sharp-pointed chin and began tugging at it thoughtfully while he went on gazing at the cake as if it could tell him something. "My guess is, you know, that the shooting happened only just before you got here. You didn't hear anything?"

"No."

"The forensic chap may say something different. Oh—" He broke off. "Here they are."

He left the kitchen and went to the front door and opened it.

Several cars had drawn up in front of the house, and a

number of men streamed into the house. Constance heard their footsteps and their voices, some exclamations of shocked surprise, a whistle or two, and even an altogether inexplicable laugh. Someone with very bad nerves, she thought. She did not know what to do with herself—stay where she was, return to the dining-room, or even go upstairs to her bedroom. She could have stayed where she was if it had not been for the cake, which seemed to be hideously mocking the tragedy that had happened in the house.

In the end, she returned to the dining-room, slipping as unobtrusively as she could through the hall, which was full of large men who looked at her with an air of wondering curiosity, but did not speak to her, and once in the dining-room, she closed the door and helped herself to more brandy.

It was only when she had been sitting there for some minutes that she noticed that there was a telephone in the room, with a directory beside it. Some more minutes passed before she suddenly got up and moving softly as if she were afraid of being caught out in doing something that was not allowable, she went to the telephone. Picking up the directory, she turned its pages till she found the number of Jenny's Café, Long Meldon. When she dialled, the telephone gave a tinkle, and she thought it might bring someone to see what she was doing and wondered if it would be considered improper. The presence of police in the house gave her a feeling of irrational guilt, although she had felt something far worse than that before their arrival.

She heard the ringing tone on the telephone, and after a moment someone said, "Jenny's Café. Can I help you?"

"Can I speak to Miss Hyland?" she said. "Miss Jennifer Hyland."

"I'm sorry, she isn't in," the voice replied. "Can I take a message for her?"

"When do you think she'll be back?"

"I'm afraid I don't know. Who is it speaking?"

"I'm Constance Lawley. I've been working at the Barrows' house for the last few days."

"I'm Julie Hyland, Jennifer's sister. She was going up to Riverside this morning. Didn't she come?"

"Oh yes, she came. And I wanted to ask her . . . Well, I'll leave it for the moment."

"Is there something wrong with the cake?"

"Oh no, it looks perfect."

"I'm sorry I can't tell you when she'll be back. I expected her some time ago, but when she didn't come, I thought perhaps she'd stayed for a chat with Mrs. Barrow. She does that sometimes. She's very fond of the Barrows."

"No, she didn't do that."

"Then I don't know where she is. She must have met some other friend and gone in to have a drink with her or something. She knows I'm here to keep an eye on things."

"Well, when she does come in, would you tell her . . ." But again it seemed impossible to leave any message for Jennifer, though it might not have been so difficult to talk to her directly. "Just ask her to ring up here when she gets in, will you? It's rather urgent."

"Something's wrong, isn't it?" Julie Hyland said. "You sound upset. Is there anything I can do?"

"No, no, I can't explain. But please just ask her to ring up."

"Yes, I'll do that."

Constance put the telephone down. A moment after

she had done it, the door opened and Inspector Frayne appeared in the doorway. His small, bright eyes studied her for a moment before he spoke.

"I listened to that little conversation of yours on the telephone out here in the hall," he said. "I heard it tinkle. Why was it you wanted to speak to Jennifer Hyland?"

"Wasn't it obvious?" she said. She went back to her chair and picked up her glass of brandy again. "I wanted to ask her what happened when she came here, whether she spoke to anyone or saw anyone and just when she came here. I don't know if she was coming straight here when I saw her leaving the café or if she had other deliveries to do first."

"I think that's a job you'd better leave to us," he said.

"But I can't help being curious."

"I'll tell you anything we find out, anything relevant. It looks a fairly straightforward case, though that doesn't make it any less horrible. Going by what you've told me, I understand the boy wasn't normal in the first place, and he'd had a very severe emotional shock. And that filled him with rage, against all the people who, he realised, had lied to him all his life, specially the mother who'd abandoned him, and he wanted to kill them all. It may be, you know, that if you hadn't gone out shopping this morning, you might have been one of them. You might be one of the corpses in that room. I think you can count yourself lucky."

"Will there be an inquest?"

"Of course."

"And I suppose I'll have to give evidence."

"It's probable."

"What do you want me to do now?" she asked. "Do you want me to stay here or can I go home?"

"You said you live in Bracklington, didn't you? I can't

see why you shouldn't go home, though I'd be grateful if you'd stay here for the present. Anyway, till the evening. We don't know what may come up. But I can understand it wouldn't be pleasant for you to spend the night here alone."

"I don't believe I could face it."

"Well, all right then, go home. But not just yet."

"I don't think there's any more I can tell you."

"You never know. And you say you're curious. Don't you want to hear what the Hyland girl has to say when she gets home? I'd be glad if you'd wait till . . . well, till they've finished in that room. They'll be removing the bodies presently. And we'll want an official statement from you, covering what you told me when I got here. I'm sorry, I don't want to make it difficult for you, but you're the only witness we've got at present."

She nodded, giving a sigh. "I know. And of course I want to help if I can. But unless Jennifer Hyland can tell you something more, I think you already know all there is to know about the whole thing. You'll tell me when I can go?"

"Yes."

He went out, closing the door behind him.

Constance stayed where she was, hearing the voices and the footsteps in the hall, yet feeling herself enclosed in silence in the empty dining-room. She did not think of looking at her watch to see what time it was or to keep any check on how long she sat there. Time seemed to pass very slowly until sometime in the afternoon when it suddenly struck her with a good deal of surprise that she was very hungry. The thought of eating was nauseating, yet her body was asking for food. She pondered which would be worse, to endure that need or to plunge out of the room among the men who were still busy at their job outside it and to make for the kitchen. Perhaps another hour passed before she abruptly made up her mind to set out to find herself something to eat.

She was fortunate that at the moment when she did this the little hall was empty. The door of the drawing-room still stood open, but she was careful not to look through it and so did not know if the dead still possessed the room or if they had been moved to the ambulance which she saw outside the front door, which also stood open. Going to the kitchen, she made herself a cheese sandwich and some coffee. Looking at her watch then, she saw that it was nearly five o'clock.

Eating the sandwich and drinking the coffee, she began to feel more normal than she had felt since coming back into the house that morning. She would have liked to remove the birthday cake from the table, to put it somewhere out of sight so that she would not have to go on suffering the horrible mockery of the hopeful message on it in its pretty pink icing. But since the police had not moved it, she presumed that they wanted it to stay where it was. They could not want her to stay here much longer, she thought. Soon she would be able to pack the small suitcase which she had brought with her and make for home.

As she was thinking this, someone knocked at the back door.

She went to open it. Conrad Greer stood there.

"In God's name, what's going on?" he asked in a hoarse whisper, as if he was afraid of being overheard by someone in the house.

"Of course, you don't know," Constance said, the fact that he was one of the people who certainly ought to know occurring to her for the first time. "Come in. What's that you've got there?" She pointed at a cardboard box that he was carrying carefully between both hands.

"Oh, it's just the chessmen for Colin," he answered as he stepped into the kitchen. "I thought I'd bring them along this evening so that they could be among his presents in the morning. But what's wrong, Mrs. Lawley? I went to the door on to the terrace, the way I usually come in, but the French window was locked and there was no one in the room, and then I saw a man come in and stand looking round, someone I'd never seen before, and then I saw through the window across the room that there was an ambulance outside and some more men there. What's happened. Has Dorothea been taken ill again?"

"The chessmen for Colin!" Constance gasped. "Oh God, it only needed that!"

He put the box down on the table beside the cake. "Please tell me what's happened." He was still half-whispering, which somehow made it more difficult for Constance to speak calmly than it would have been if he had spoken normally.

Sitting down, leaning her head on her hands, she said, "I haven't much experience of breaking bad news. I don't know how to set about it. But a fearful thing has happened. Colin somehow got hold of a gun this morning, and he shot his grandparents and his mother and then, it seems, himself. Those men you saw out there are police. They've been here all day, and if the drawing-room's empty now, it's because they've put the bodies into the ambulance. I think they'll be leaving soon."

"The bodies!" he exclaimed. "Colin shot them? You mean he killed them?"

"Isn't that what I said?"

"Yes, but— You can't mean that. Why would Colin do a thing like that?"

"Why does a boy like Colin do anything?"

"You do mean it!" His voice was suddenly loud.

"Yes."

"His grandparents and Margot?"

"Yes, yes, yes!" For the moment she felt wildly impatient with him because he was being so slow, taking it in. But then she recognized how hard it would have been for her to believe what had happened if she had not walked into the dreadful room and seen it for herself. When she spoke again, her voice was gentle. "He was your son, wasn't he?"

He nodded and seemed about to say something, but paused and then asked, "Who's in charge here?"

"A man called Frayne."

"I'd better go and talk to him."

He turned towards the door, but as he did so, it opened and Inspector Frayne came into the kitchen. Seeing Greer, he looked questioningly at Constance, waiting to have the presence of this man explained.

She said, "This is Mr. Greer, a neighbour."

"Greer?" the inspector said. "Anything to do with the Greer who owns the antique shop in Bracklington?"

"Yes," Greer said shortly.

"That's who you are? Come to think of it, someone told me you lived in Long Meldon—I can't remember who at the moment. What's this?" He put his hands on the cardboard box on the table.

"Leave that!" Greer said. "It was just something for the boy's birthday. Please don't touch it."

But Frayne had already lifted the lid and was looking into the box.

"Chessmen," he said softly. "That might be interesting."

Five

For a moment after that, neither of the men said anything. Frayne went on looking at the box. Greer looked at him with an expression of deep shock on his face. Then Frayne put the lid back on the box and picked it up.

Greer exclaimed, "Leave that! It's nothing to do with you."

"If that's true, it'll be returned to you undamaged," Frayne said equably.

"You're meaning to take it away with you?" Greer asked.

"Probably."

"I'm sure you've no right to do that. I'm sure you've no right. You don't believe it's got anything to do with this ghastly thing that's happened here, do you? How could it? I've only just heard about it."

"All the same, it could be interesting."

"Why?"

"The boy played chess, didn't he?"

"Yes."

"And those were a present for him?"

"Yes, but I still don't understand why you want to take them away. They're quite valuable, you know."

"I rather thought they might be. Where did they come from?"

"That's none of your business. I had them; I thought I'd give them to him. But he's dead, so I'll take them home again."

The antagonism between the two men was quiet but intense, and to Constance, it seemed to be growing. Shrinking from it, feeling that Greer was incomprehensibly upset and that an explosion resulting from this would be just more than she could bear, she said, "I wouldn't make a fuss about it, Mr. Greer. I don't know why Inspector Frayne wants them, but I'm sure you'll get them back all right."

"Thank you, Mrs. Lawley," Frayne said. "I promise that. But I'd like to know where you got them, Mr. Greer."

"They've been in my shop for some time," Greer answered. "I forget where I got them."

"You bought them from someone, I suppose."

"Naturally."

"But you don't remember who?"

"No."

"Don't you keep records of that sort of thing?"

"There's probably a record in my books in the shop, but I don't carry it around in my head."

"Well, I'll call in at the shop sometime. Perhaps you can check your records meanwhile."

"I suppose so," Greer said grudgingly. "But I still don't understand why you're interested in them. Colonel Barrow seemed to think they weren't the right sort of thing to give a boy like Colin, and I nearly changed my mind about giving them to him; but I hadn't anything else and it was a bit late to go shopping, so I took the risk of giving them to him all the same."

"Ah, so you thought there was some risk about doing it."

It appeared to be another question to which Greer did not immediately know the answer.

At length he said, in a more propitiatory tone than he had yet used in this argument, "I'm always scared about giving presents. If you can see they aren't liked, if you've made a blunder choosing them, it can hurt quite a bit. Colonel Barrow seemed to think Colin might not value them and might even smash them."

"But you didn't think he'd really do that, or you wouldn't have brought them."

"Just so."

"All the same, you've known him to be violent, have you? Has he smashed things before?"

"Colonel Barrow told me once about a teddy bear he'd cut up with a razor. But that was long ago. I've never seen him violent myself."

"Can you believe he killed his grandparents and his mother?"

Greer seemed to take this question more calmly than he had those about the chessmen. He moved towards a chair and sat down, gazing before him with unfocussed eyes, as if he hoped to find the answer in the empty air before him.

"I've got to believe it, haven't I?" he said in a low voice. "Mrs. Lawley told me that's what happened. Is there any other explanation possible?"

"It's still too soon to say," Frayne answered. "That's what it looks like. But can you believe it of him?"

"I suppose so. If he was badly enough upset. He had very unpredictable moods."

"He seems to have been very upset by the arrival of his mother and the man I suppose one should call his stepfather."

"Wouldn't any child be? He'd believed all his life his mother was dead."

"But not every child would know where to lay his hands on a gun. Do you know if Colonel Barrow kept a gun in the house?"

"Yes, as it happens I do. He showed it to me once. I think it was a memento of his days in India."

"So Colin probably knew about it."

"He must have."

"Yes, well thank you, Mr. Greer. It's useful to know about the gun. By the way, you've known the Barrows a long time, have you?"

"Oh yes."

"Before they moved to Long Meldon?"

"Yes. As a matter of fact, it was I who found them this house. They'd just taken on Colin and they talked to me about wanting to move into the country, as they thought it would be the best thing for him, and I happened to know this house was coming on to the market and I told them about it."

"I see. Well, we'll be in touch again soon." Suddenly moving rapidly, Frayne picked up the box of chessmen and, almost as if he felt that Greer might follow and snatch it from him, shot out of the kitchen.

The moment he had gone, Greer, startled by the swiftness of it, broke into an explosion of curses, which seemed to relate to the abduction of the chessmen rather than to anything else.

"But it doesn't really matter, does it?" Constance said. "I suppose he's got to investigate everything that could conceivably have anything to do with Colin, but he'll soon see these couldn't possibly and he'll bring them back to you."

Greer drew a deep breath and let it out slowly. He seemed to be making a deliberate effort to relax, yet when he looked at Constance, she thought that there was still a strange gleam of fear in his eyes.

"I can't help wondering . . ." he began, but then paused.

"Yes?" Constance said.

"No, it's absurd." He drew a hand across his forehead temporarily smoothing out the deep lines that had appeared there. "I was just wondering if Godfrey could have told Colin about the chessmen and how he'd advised me not to give them to him, and could that have made Colin furious, because he wanted them. I think I showed them to him once when Dorothea brought him into the shop one day. She rather liked coming in and picking up knick-knacks. No, it's absurd."

Constance thought that it was absurd too. Furthermore, she did not believe it was what Greer had started to say when he stated that there was something that he could not help wondering about. He could not even momentarily have imagined that the murderous impulse that had moved Colin had been prompted by the deprivation of some chessmen that he had fancied. She looked curiously at Greer, wondering what it was that he was trying so hard to hide. He had not told Frayne that he was Colin's father and that once, many years ago, he had had a close relationship with Margot Pauling. But that was something which in these days there was no great need to conceal.

He stood up, looking at the birthday cake, and said, "I'd like to smash that bloody thing to pieces."

"So would I, rather," Constance said.

"Are you staying the night here?" he asked.

"No, I'm going home."

"I don't blame you. Well, I'll be off home myself. If there's anything I can do, you'll let me know, won't you?"

"Thank you, yes. But I don't think they'll want me for anything more."

"Goodbye, then."

"Goodbye."

He let himself out of the back door.

If Constance had not felt as tired as she did, she would have got up then and gone in search of Inspector Frayne to ask if there was any reason why she should remain in the house. The thought of her own had never seemed so attractive. But lethargy, the aftermath of emotions to which she was wholly unaccustomed, kept her passively where she was.

She could not guess why the detective had been so interested in the chessmen and had so relentlessly taken possession of them. They seemed to her as irrelevant as the things which she had bought in the village that morning and which, she realised with slight surprise, she had not yet put away. Wearily she got up and started putting them into the refrigerator. But was there any point in bothering with this? she wondered. There was no one left in the house who would ever again be requiring food. In a little while everything in the refrigerator would have to be emptied into the dustbin. But wasting food was one of the things of which she was incapable.

She had just closed the door of the refrigerator on her purchases when Frayne came back into the kitchen.

She imagined that it would be to tell her that she could go home, but he said, "You're wanted on the telephone."

"I am?" she said, believing that there was no one who would think of telephoning her here. Then she wondered if it could be Pauling.

"Yes," Frayne said. "Will you take it in the dining-room?"

"While you listen in in the hall?"

"Do you mind?"

"You'd do it whether I mind or not, wouldn't you?" she said. "And I imagine it's best for me if you do it. You'll know I haven't some secret ploy going on. But I wish I understood what you want with those chessmen."

"Fingerprints, for one thing."

"But what can they tell you? There'll be all sorts of people's prints on them, won't there?"

"That remains to be seen. But I shouldn't keep this lady on the telephone waiting."

"It's a lady, is it?"

"That's right."

She went to the dining-room, picked up the telephone, and said, "Constance Lawley speaking".

"Oh, Mrs. Lawley, this is Julie Hyland," a voice said. "I wanted to ask you about Jennifer. Is she with you?"

"No," Constance replied.

"Has she been with you any time today?"

"No. But she came here in the morning. I know that because she delivered Colin's birthday cake. But I was out at the time."

"But you're sure she did that?"

"Yes, it's here. It was she who delivered it, I suppose; it couldn't have been anyone else?"

"No, it must have been Jennifer. Anyway, she took it with her when she left here, and I can't imagine she'd have handed it over to someone else to make the actual delivery. But you haven't seen her?"

"No. But, Miss Hyland, do you know about what's happened here today?"

There was a slight pause; then Julie's voice, with a slight shake in it, went on, "Yes, the police came here this afternoon because they wanted to speak to Jennifer, and they told me the whole awful story. I believe it was you who walked in on it and found . . . everything. It must have been an unspeakable shock for you."

"It was."

"I'm . . . I'm so sorry—for you, I mean, and for all of them. But I always felt that boy Colin was sooner or later going to turn out to be dangerous. I didn't think anyone took his mental condition nearly seriously enough."

"It looks as if you were right."

"Nobody listened to me, though. They all knew he didn't like me, and I suppose when I tried to warn them, as I did, they thought I was just getting my own back. I think it was really the other way round—I mean, that he didn't like me because he knew what I thought of him. Conrad adored the little horror. Of course, you know he was his son."

"That's what Mr. Pauling told me."

"Oh, it's true. You'd only to look at them to see the resemblance. But about Jennifer, Mrs. Lawley, actually I'm getting rather worried about her. It isn't at all like her to stay away for most of the day without telling me she was going to do it. Do you think I ought to tell the police about it?"

"I don't think there's any need to do that," Constance said, "because they're listening in on this line."

"Oh!" There was a sound of shock in it; then there was a pause, as if Julie were trying to assess whether or not this mattered. Then she went on, "That simplifies

matters, of course. So they're still in the house with
you."

"Yes."

"You're staying the night there, are you?"

"No, I'm going home."

"I was hoping I could come up and have a talk with
you. I've a feeling the police didn't tell me everything—
and if they're listening in now and heard me say that, it
doesn't matter, does it? How much longer will you be
there?"

"I don't know. Anyway, I can wait for you if you
want to come. There's something I'd rather like to ask
you . . ." But the thought of the listener on the line
checked her. "Well, I can ask you about it when you get
here."

"I'll be along quite soon, then. Meanwhile, if you
hear anything from Jennifer, you'll let me know, won't
you?"

"Of course."

Constance heard her ring off and put down the telephone that she was holding. The question that she had
nearly asked Julie had concerned the chessmen. If they
had come from the antique shop in Bracklington, Julie
very probably knew where they had come from in the
first place and when Conrad Greer had removed them
from the shop and what connection, if any, they could
have with the morning's crimes. She thought that
Frayne was an intelligent man and that his interest in
the chessmen could not be without significance, but
what significance it had puzzled her very much and she
did not like being puzzled.

The police left the house soon afterwards, Frayne telling Constance that she was free to go home when she
liked, but that he would like her to be available there
next day as he would still require a formal statement

from her. She had been longing for all the men to leave, yet as soon as they had gone, the emptiness and silence of the house became almost unbearable. She wished that she had not given Julie the promise to wait for her to come. If only she had thought faster, she could have suggested that she would call in on Jenny's Café on her way home. Since Jennifer was more likely to return there than to come to Riverside, it would really have been a far more sensible arrangement than to wait here. She might still do that, she thought. She could telephone the café and suggest to Julie that she should wait there for Constance to come.

When she telephoned, however, there was no reply. The café, she supposed, was already closed for the evening and Julie was on her way here, and only a moment after putting the telephone down Constance heard the front door bell ring. Going to answer it, she assumed that it would be Julie who was there, but with a slight start of surprise, she saw that it was Kenneth Pauling.

He noticed the start and said, "I'm afraid you weren't expecting me. But may I come in? I know what happened to Margot and the others, but if you wouldn't mind . . . I know it sounds morbid, but I've an awful desire to see where it happened and to ask you a few things. But if you'd sooner I went away, I'll go."

"It's only that I was expecting someone else," Constance said, "and that I'm meaning to go home as soon as I can. And I'm afraid you can't see the actual room where it happened, because I'm afraid they've put seals on the door. I suppose they mean to come back tomorrow, though I'm not sure what for. The whole tragic thing seems to be quite simple in its awful way. But come in and have a drink. I've no work to do this evening and I'm not in any hurry to go anywhere."

He followed her inside and then stood still in the hall, looking at the closed door of the drawing-room.

"It was in there, was it?" he asked.

"Yes," she answered. She hesitated for a moment, uncertain where to take him, and then led him into the dining-room. The bottle of brandy from which she had helped herself in the morning, was still on the table. "Brandy?" she said. "Or whisky, or sherry?"

"Whisky, please, with soda, if you've got it." Going to the window, he stood there, gazing out. The daylight was beginning to lose its brilliance, though it was not yet dusk. Beyond the terrace a lawn sloped away between wide herbaceous borders towards a copse of beeches and the river Meldon. "It looks so peaceful, doesn't it?" he said. "It's hard to take in what's happened here. I told you I knew about it. The police came to see me this afternoon, asked me questions about my relationship with Margot, then wanted me to go to the morgue to identify her. I've been walking round in a sort of daze ever since. Do you think it would have happened if I hadn't come here? Was it my coming that pushed the boy over the edge?"

Constance poured out whisky for him and after some hesitation a small brandy for herself. Even that, she thought, might be unwise, since she was intending to drive into Bracklington shortly, and as she had had hardly anything to eat all day, the drink, she knew, would go to her head. But she wanted it badly and thought that after all, if she felt unsure of herself, she could stay overnight in this house. Now that the police had gone and she was becoming more used to the silence of the place, the idea of staying there no longer seemed so frightening.

"It's useless to ask oneself that sort of question," she said. "A little while ago I was asking myself if it was my fault because I didn't take Colin seriously when he told me he meant to kill everybody. Perhaps it was my fault, but blaming myself now isn't going to help anybody."

He turned towards the table and picked up the whisky and soda that she had poured out for him.

"I suppose there's no doubt it was the boy who killed them all," he said.

"I don't think there's any question of it," she answered.

"Somehow I can't believe it."

"Oh, I've that feeling too. Really terrible things only happen to other people, don't they? One doesn't get involved in them oneself."

"I suppose there's no one else who had any motive to kill them all," he said.

She wrinkled her forehead, looking at him, wondering how serious he was. He did not meet her eyes, but looked down at his drink. His square face had a closed, aloof expression on it.

"I can't imagine anyone wanting to kill Colonel and Mrs. Barrow except for some utterly irrational reason," she said. "They were quiet, kind people. I'm sure they never did anyone any harm in their lives. And they weren't rich. Comfortably off, but not affluent. I don't know of anyone who stood to inherit much by their deaths. I suppose at present-day prices this house alone is worth a good deal, but Colonel Barrow's pension will stop. Perhaps they had a certain amount in investments, but actually, since Margot and Colin are both dead too, I don't know who will inherit."

"You know, it might be me," Pauling said, still looking at his drink with that air of abstraction, then suddenly gulping half of it.

"You? Oh, because they may have left their money to

Margot, and she may have made a will, leaving what she had to you?"

He nodded. "She did that. We both made wills, leaving everything we had to each other."

"But suppose the Barrows left everything they had to Colin."

"Oh yes, I'm not thinking of making a claim to their property. All the same, it may come to me, and if I'd heard that it would, it would have given me a possible motive for killing the two old people, along with Margot and Colin. And as it happens, I'm in need of money."

"I thought you had a good job in Sydney," Constance said.

"So I had until a month ago, when the firm I've been working for went bust. And so far I haven't been able to find anything else. And Margot's business never made much money. It was more something to give her an interest than really a paying proposition."

"What was it exactly?"

"Interior decorating. She was pretty gifted at it, and from time to time she'd pull off a big deal and suddenly be flush. But it was nothing to count on."

"Who's looking after it now?"

"An assistant she had, I presume, unless she simply walked out on it. A young woman who came into the business a couple of years ago. But I don't think she's experienced enough to take it over and I certainly couldn't, and if we simply sell up our stock, it won't bring in much. Oh, I could do with a couple of hundred thousand, which I imagine is the sort of sum this house will fetch. Don't you think it's fortunate for me that I've got an alibi for the time of the killings?"

He looked up to meet her eyes now with a humourless smile.

"Are you thinking of our having coffee together around the time they happened?" Constance asked.

"You're a little quick for me, but yes, that had occurred to me," he said.

"And that's why you really came up here this evening. It was to make sure I'd corroborate that."

"Actually, no. It was only when you began to talk about the person who was going to inherit the Barrows' money that I realised it might be me and that that gave me a motive for wiping out the family. And so I thought of that coffee we had together and felt rather glad we'd had it."

"What did you do after we separated?"

"I went for a stroll through the village, then went back to the Green Dragon and had a drink, then some lunch—" He stopped abruptly and the thick eyebrows over his light brown eyes twitched frowningly together. "Look, you aren't seriously asking me for my alibi, are you?"

"It was you who introduced the subject," she said.

"True, but I was merely exploring it theoretically, seeing if a case could be made out against me if the police should start to wonder if Colin really committed all those murders."

"But I can't really support your alibi, you know." The brandy was giving Constance a feeling that she was thinking remarkably clearly. "When I left you, I went into the grocer's, and I was there quite a long time. And the murders are supposed to have happened only a very short time before I got in, so if you'd set off for this house immediately we parted, you just might have been able to get here and carry out the shootings before I arrived."

"Seems to me I'd have had to walk at a hell of a pace, which would probably have attracted attention to me as

I went. There'd be witnesses to tell the police about it, but I'm not really afraid of them. I've no car, you know. I'd have had to come on foot."

"But you didn't talk to anyone after you left me? There's no one who'd be able to say for sure where you were?"

He gave a harsh little laugh. "I wonder if this is a rehearsal for the questions the police may be asking me tomorrow. If so, it may be useful. I realise I'd better do some thinking."

"You know, you still haven't told me your real reason for coming here this evening," Constance said. "Was it really to have a look at the room where it all happened?"

He did not answer at once, but leaning his head on a hand, let his frown disappear and a look of faint amusement take its place.

"You're in the wrong job, aren't you?" he said. "Someone like you could be very useful to the police. No, it wasn't really to have a look at the room. It was mainly to talk to you. I'd got to talk to someone. I tried sitting in my room with a book, but I couldn't bear it, so I thought I'd come here and perhaps you'd offer me a drink, as you did, and we could chat for a time and things wouldn't seem so awful and impossible as they were doing. But, on the whole, it seems to have been a mistake. This chat hasn't been exactly reassuring."

"But it's you who made out the case against yourself —" she broke off as the door bell rang.

He quickly emptied his glass and stood up.

"If that's the police again . . ."

"I don't think it is," Constance said. "I think it's Miss Hyland. If you remember, we met her in the café this morning. She's worried about her sister."

She left the dining-room and went to open the front door.

Julie Hyland stood there. She did not look as stern and self-assured as she had in the morning, and the fair hair that then had been sleekly drawn back from her face had a wind-blown look, although there was no wind blowing that evening. It might be that she had been thrusting her fingers through it. She had on a light jacket over her cotton dress and had her hands thrust down into its pockets.

"Have you any news?" she asked.

"About Jennifer? No," Constance answered. "But why should you think I might have? Why should she come here?"

"I don't know. I don't know anything. I don't suppose she would. It's just that I'm feeling scared and more than a bit desperate. I feel I ought to be doing something. Don't you think I ought to tell the police that she still hasn't come home?"

"Well, come in," Constance said. "Join Mr. Pauling and me in a drink. None of us know what we ought to be doing. I think the answer is, nothing. But come in."

Julie Hyland stepped into the hall and followed Constance to the dining-room. Pauling was standing where Constance had left him. He gave Julie a slightly puzzled scrutiny, as if he knew that they had met before but could not for the moment remember where.

Then his face cleared and he said, "Ah yes, this morning in the café."

Constance introduced them, "Miss Hyland, Mr. Pauling. What will you have to drink, Miss Hyland?"

"For God's sake, call me Julie. Whisky, please." Julie sank into a chair, sitting limply there as if she were very tired, yet looking at Pauling as if something about him were deeply interesting to her.

"You're Margot's husband," she said as Constance put a glass of whisky in front of her.

"Yes," he said.

"Then what's happened is very terrible for you. Specially terrible."

"I think you may say that."

Constance gave Pauling some more whisky and poured out some more brandy for herself. As she did it, she made up her mind that she would not drive home that evening. The brandy was very comforting. It made her feel that there was nothing seriously wrong with her world. And that meant, she thought, that she could not be really fit to be on the road.

Julie turned to her.

"I can't understand it," she said. "Jennifer went off this morning to deliver Colin's cake. I thought she was going to come straight back. Then at first, when she didn't come, I thought she must have stayed here to have coffee and a chat with Mrs. Barrow. And even when she didn't come home in time for lunch, I thought she might have stayed on or met some other friend perhaps. But when the police came and told me what had happened here, I really began to worry. You see, it isn't like Jennifer to go off without any idea when she'd be back, and if for some reason she'd suddenly decided to go into Bracklington shopping or something of that sort, she'd probably have telephoned. But it's getting late now and she still hasn't come home. So what can I do about it?"

"Just why did the police come to see you this afternoon?" Pauling asked. "Why did they connect you with things here?"

"Because of the cake, of course," Julie answered. "It was Jennifer they wanted to see, not me. They knew she'd been here because the cake had been delivered,

and I suppose they wanted to know if she'd seen anything unusual."

"And do you think she had?" he asked.

"How on earth can I tell?" Her voice rose momentarily with the shrillness of hysteria in it, but then she
carefully controlled it and in a level tone went on, "I
can't help thinking it looks like it. But even if she did,
why did she have to vanish? Suppose she actually saw
that boy Colin shoot everyone and then himself and she
couldn't stop him, why didn't she simply ring the police immediately? She'd have no reason to run away."

"Shock, perhaps," he suggested.

She gave a bewildered frown. "Is that really possible?"

"I believe it might be," he said. "If she saw something as terrible as what happened, she might have had
a complete black-out and be wandering around, not
knowing where she is or even who she is."

"She was in her car," Julie said. "The police didn't
find it here, so she must have driven away in it. And
she'd have had her handbag with her and there'd have
been her banker's card in it and her cheque-book and so
on, so when she came to, she could have checked up
. . . Oh, you think perhaps she hasn't come to yet! If
there's any possibility of that, I've got to get in touch
with the police and tell them she still hasn't come
home, haven't I?"

"I think I would," Constance said.

"Can I use that telephone there?"

"Yes, go ahead."

But Julie did not rise immediately to go to the telephone. Sipping her whisky, she looked thoughtfully at
Pauling.

"You and your wife were the Paulings in Sydney who

sometimes bought antiques from Conrad Greer, were you?"

"Did Margot do that?" he asked. "I didn't know anything about that side of her business. She certainly got some very nice pieces from Europe from time to time."

"Oh yes, it was one of my jobs to see to the dispatching of them, but the name Pauling didn't mean anything to me. I didn't connect it with a daughter of the Barrows. But your wife was an old friend of Conrad's, wasn't she?"

"So I believe." His tone was expressionless.

"But you didn't know she was still in contact with him. Oh yes, she was a good customer of ours. I work for him, you know. Now if you don't mind, Mrs. Lawley, I'll telephone."

Julie got up and went to the telephone, picked up the directory, and looked for the number of the Bracklington police. When she had dialled and was answered, she said that she wanted to report a missing person. She spoke calmly, identifying herself, explaining her connection with the murders in Long Meldon and her fear that her sister might have seen them and, in a state of shock, be wandering about, suffering from loss of memory. Constance, listening, realised that at a certain point Julie had been connected with Detective Inspector Frayne, for after a slight break she started repeating all that she had already said.

When she put the telephone down, she said, "They're putting out an alert, or whatever they call it, about her. I suppose they'll find her. Meanwhile, there doesn't seem to be anything more I can do. I may as well go home. Thank you for listening to me, Mrs. Lawley. Do you want a lift back to the village, Mr. Pauling? I've got my car here."

"Thank you," he said, "if it isn't any trouble to you."

"Shall we go then?"

He and Julie left together. Constance, who by then had decided to stay the night in the house, went to the front door with them and closed it after them. It disturbed her in a way that she did not understand to see them walking together towards Julie's car. From the moment when Julie had spoken of Margot buying antiques from Conrad Greer and Pauling had answered her so flatly, she had felt that there was something between them, some kind of secret knowledge perhaps and certainly hostility, which brought a complexity into their relationship about which she did not want to have to think just then.

She did not want to think about anything at all. She wanted to finish her brandy, find something to eat for her supper, and go to bed. Finding some cold lamb in the refrigerator, she cut up a tomato and made a slice of bread and butter, and listlessly and only half aware of what she was doing, sat down at the kitchen table, ate her snack, and then went wearily upstairs. Within a few minutes of getting into bed she was in a deep and dreamless sleep.

The sound of the telephone ringing woke her.

At first she was only drowsily aware of it and, because she was a guest in a house that belonged to other people, did not feel that there was any need for her to answer it. Then remembrance of the day before came flooding back, and grabbing her dressing-gown and struggling into it as she went, she hurried down the stairs to the telephone in the hall. But the ringing had stopped by the time that she reached it.

Sleepily she went into the kitchen and made coffee. Why on earth, she wondered, had she stayed on the

evening before instead of going home. The real reason
for it, she supposed, was that she had simply not felt up
to it. The brandy had been part of it, but most of it had
been nervous exhaustion. But there was no real reason
why she should not go home this morning. She had just
started on her second cup of coffee when the telephone
rang again.

"Is that you, Mum?" a voice said when she answered.
"This is Irene."

"Irene? Goodness me, how did you know where I
was?" Constance asked.

"You wrote to me, remember?" Irene said. "I got the
letter yesterday morning."

"I didn't know the Royal Mail did anything as fast as
that nowadays," Constance said. "One wouldn't expect
you to have got my letter till tomorrow at the earliest."

"It is a bit surprising," Irene agreed. "But look, is it
true you're in the house where that fearful massacre
happened? Riverside—you mean you're really in a
house called Riverside, do you?"

There was a degree of concern in Irene's voice to
which Constance was not accustomed.

"Yes, but how did you know about that?" she asked.

"It was on the seven o'clock news. I didn't believe it.
Then I thought I'd better ring up and find out. Mum, it
sounds terrible. Aren't you terrified?"

"Fairly terrified, yes," Constance answered, "though
it's stupid, because I wasn't even in the house when it
happened and it's all over now except for the police
coming and going. Was that you trying to phone me a
little while ago?"

"Yes, and when I didn't get any answer, I rang the
house in Bracklington, in case you'd gone home since
you wrote, and then when I got no answer, I thought
I'd try this number again in case there'd been some-

thing wrong with the line or you were having a bath or something. You're all right, are you, Mum? I mean, the shock must have been fearful, and after all, you aren't used to that kind of thing."

"I can't say I've ever experienced anything quite like it before," Constance said, "but I think I've managed to keep my head."

"That's fine. I mean, I knew you would, because you always keep your head in almost any circumstances, but I'm glad you've been able to face things. Living the sort of life you do, knowing from one day to the next just what's going to happen, it must have been specially shattering."

"One never knows what's going to happen tomorrow, however humdrum one's existence seems to be. But you think your rather different experience of life would have fitted you to cope with the situation better than me."

"Now don't go all sarcastic on me, Mum," Irene said. "Of course not. I'd have run from the house screaming, whereas I'm sure you did the proper thing and dialled 999. But I'm so afraid you'll pay for it later. I mean, keeping your head in a crisis often means that you'll feel ten times worse later on than if you let your feelings rip at the time. Not that I don't admire you for being able to do it. But I think I'd better come down in case you need some help presently. You'll be staying on at that house in Long Meldon, will you?"

"Now, please, Irene," Constance said quickly, "don't think of coming down. It's very sweet of you to think of it, but I really don't need any help."

She certainly did not need any help, she thought, of the kind that Irene could give her.

"Oh, that's all right," Irene said. "I'll come. I'm not sure what the trains are, but I'll go to Paddington and

take the next one. Sunday trains are pretty bad, but I
expect I'll arrive some time this morning."

"Please, Irene, don't . . . I'm not even sure if I'll be
staying here."

"Don't worry about that. If you aren't at Long Meldon, I'll go on into Bracklington. I can afford a taxi. I've
got quite a lot of money, because I've got a job. And I
really don't like the thought of you having to cope with
the police all by yourself. Have they been awful?"

"The police?"

"Yes."

"The man in charge here has been very courteous and
considerate."

"That's what they're sometimes like to begin with.
You don't know what may happen next. Well, I'll be
down later this morning, and meanwhile, try not to get
too depressed and all that sort of thing."

Constance heard the click of the telephone being put
down.

"Oh dear . . ." she murmured. She was not sure if
she felt more touched at Irene's unexpected concern for
her, astonished at the statement that she had a job, or
appalled at the thought of her interfering in Constance's quite good relationship with Inspector Frayne.

Her next ordeal was the press. She had just got
dressed when they started arriving. They came with
notebooks, with cameras, with questions, some of them
putting to her the one that she had always thought
most supremely impertinent when she had heard it on
radio or television. How had she *felt*, they wanted to
know, when she had walked into a room and found
four dead bodies in it. She tried replying that she considered her feelings strictly private and thought that
ought to put an end to the matter, but the questions
came again and again—what had been her *feelings*

when she discovered the tragedy. Shock, she admitted now, wanting at any price to be left to herself, terrible shock, and added that she really had no words in which to express what she had felt. They nodded and scribbled in their notebooks and exuded a little synthetic sympathy, but seemed satisfied and strolled off. Thinking that they had really had no need to interview her at all, because they could safely have made up for themselves anything that she had told them, she closed the door on them, went up to her bedroom, and began to pack her suitcase.

The front door bell rang.

She was not much surprised to find Inspector Frayne on the doorstep. She had felt that she had not seen the last of him.

"So you stayed after all," he said as he stepped into the hall.

"Yes, but I'm going home now, if you don't mind," she said.

"Well, I'm not sure," he said as she took him into the dining-room. "It might be a good thing if you stayed on. But it's up to you to decide. It's just that it looks at the moment as if you may be about the last person to have seen Jennifer Hyland alive."

"Alive . . . ?" she exclaimed. "You don't mean . . ."

"I'm afraid I do," he said. "We found her this morning. If you go straight on up this lane past Mr. Greer's house, you come a mile or so further on to a place where the river widens into a small pool. And a man coming down the lane about eight o'clock noticed a car among the trees there, and because there's no track or any obvious reason why a car should be parked where it was, he went to take a look at it. It was empty, but there was a body in the pool. Drowned, he thought. Suicide. But it's turned out that she'd been violently struck on the head before she drowned, so after all, the probability is that it's murder."

Six

Constance was shocked at the first thought that came
into her mind as she listened. It was that in her last job,
where her employers had objected to all food that was
not grown organically and to eggs that had not been laid
by free-range fowls, there had been no hint of violence
in their home, no mystery, no murder. Trying to do the
housekeeping of a kind that they would accept had at
times been difficult, but how peaceful it had been, how
secure it had felt.

"But why?" she said.

"Why was she murdered?"

"Yes."

"There are several possible reasons," Frayne answered. He dropped into a chair at the table and sat
there in the drooping attitude of extreme weariness.
Constance wondered if he had had any sleep that night.
"One, did she pick up a hitch-hiker who killed her,

stole her handbag, and made off? However, she hadn't been raped; that's one thing we know."

"But her handbag's missing, is it?" Constance said.

"Yes, but we found it in a ditch at the edge of the lane, with only the money she'd had in it missing."

"Was she carrying much money?"

"We've been talking to her sister, and she thinks probably not. But that doesn't necessarily mean anything. Murders have been done for as little as thirty pence."

"What other reasons are there?"

"There's the one that stares one in the face. She came here with the birthday cake, saw something, and had to be put out of the way."

Constance, who had sat down facing him, felt a chill go through her.

"That doesn't make sense, does it?" she said. "If Jennifer saw Colin shooting his grandparents and his mother and then himself, he couldn't have done her any harm, could he?"

"No," he agreed. "If you put it like that, probably not."

"Why only probably not? Why not certainly not?" She looked searchingly into his bright blue eyes, which this morning looked duller than she had yet seen them. "What do you really believe?"

"If you want to hide a leaf," he said, "where would you put it?"

"Oh, I know the answer to that one—in a forest," she replied.

"And if you want to hide a corpse?"

"On a battlefield, I presume."

"But suppose there's no convenient little war going on in your neighbourhood, what then?"

Her gaze on his tired face changed from being merely

curious to suddenly intent and more than a little scared.

"I think I understand what you mean," she said. "You suspect that at least one of the people in that room yesterday wasn't killed by Colin. That someone who saw what Colin was doing took the opportunity of adding another corpse to the slaughter. And Jennifer saw it happen."

"Well, what do you think of it?" he asked.

She shut her eyes, trying to visualise what might have happened in the pleasant drawing-room while she had been out shopping. It might have been something even more horrific and much more bewildering than she had yet imagined.

"I can think of one argument against it," she said after a long pause.

"I'd be glad to hear it."

"It's a question of time. I think it was about half past ten when I went to Jenny's Café to have a cup of coffee with Mr. Pauling. And as we went in, we saw Jennifer setting out in her car. Her sister, Julie, says she believed Jennifer was just going to deliver the cake here . . . Oh God!" she stopped.

"What is it?" Frayne asked.

"Just that I've remembered today was Colin's birthday. The cake and the chessmen and I believe a camera were all for him. I hadn't thought of that till this moment."

"It isn't the pleasantest of thoughts. But what were you going to say about Jennifer Hyland delivering the cake?"

"Only that if she'd come straight here, she'd have arrived at say a quarter to eleven at the latest. But I believe your people think the murder happened only very shortly before I got in and that can't have been much before half past eleven at the very earliest. I told you, after Mr. Pauling and I had had our coffee, I did some shopping and I took quite a time about it. So if Jennifer saw something like a murder done by someone who wasn't Colin and was killed because of what she'd seen, what was she doing between the time she got here and the time the murders were done? If she'd simply been sitting here, chatting to Mrs. Barrow when the shootings began, she'd have been killed here too, wouldn't she? She wouldn't have been driven up the lane and hit over the head and drowned in a pool there, at great risk, I'd say, to whoever did it. She'd simply have been left in the carnage here."

He nodded. "I thought you'd say that."

"Doesn't it make sense?"

"Oh yes. Yes, very much so. And it means it's important to account for what she was doing for about the half hour or so after you saw her drive away from the café. We've got men out making inquiries about that now. The answer may be something quite simple—for instance, that she dropped in on a friend for a chat before she came up here and so just happened to be on the spot when the extra murder happened."

"You're really sure there was an extra murder, are you?"

"Oh no, not sure."

"But it's what you believe, isn't it?"

"I'm inclined to believe it. But it could have been something else she saw, not a murder. For instance, someone might have been looking on and saw the murders were going to happen and didn't interfere. That could be a very serious criminal offence. Someone might even have encouraged the boy to do what we think he did. If she was a witness to that, it might be worth that person's while to get rid of her."

"They'd have had to see it through the French window on to the terrace, wouldn't they?"

"That's probable."

"And the person who had a way of coming in and out of the house that way was Conrad Greer. And you've impounded his chessmen. That still puzzles me. Have they told you anything?"

"Only that they were stolen."

"Stolen!" She drew a deep breath, let it out in a slow sigh, and shook her head. "I don't understand. Do you mean by Conrad Greer?"

"Oh, not necessarily," he said. "He may have bought them in good faith. Buying stolen goods is one of the risks all antique dealers run. His deciding to give them as a present to the boy suggests that he didn't know they were stolen. If he had known it, he'd have realised what a risk he was running by doing it."

"How do you know they were stolen?"

"There are some fingerprints on several of the pieces which indicate that they were formerly the property of a certain Lady Bancroft who lives in Granwich, that village about ten miles the other side of Bracklington. You probably know it. Last May she had a burglary in her house there in which, among other things, all of them reasonably valuable, a set of Chinese chessmen were stolen. We're fairly sure who took them and even what he did with them, and that was why I took possession of them when I saw them here."

"You say you're fairly sure what this person did with them."

"Of course, one can be wrong."

"But all the same, you're suspicious he sold them to Conrad Greer and that he knew what he was doing, buying them. In other words, he's a fence."

"Is that what you think yourself?"

"It's what you think, isn't it?"

"I wouldn't go so far as to say that."

"Because it would be very indiscreet if you haven't enough evidence. But I think you believe he's a fence and perhaps that his shop is only a front for other activities, and you're about ready to pounce on him for it any time now. I'd like to know if you think the Paulings are involved."

"The Paulings?" he said with raised eyebrows. He looked unable to follow her.

"Yes, both of whom are here now," she said. "One dead, one alive. And who, according to Julie Hyland, were good customers of Conrad Greer's. Margot Pauling ran an interior decorating business in Sydney, and a supply of good antiques from Europe may have been very useful to her. But did she know that what she was getting had been stolen? Apart from that, suppose you tell me something else: why did you come to see me this morning?"

He gave a slight shrug of his shoulders.

"Partly to have the sort of talk we've been having. That's to say, to find out if you knew anything that might be useful, even if you hadn't realised it yourself. Like this Pauling connection, for instance. No doubt we'd have got around to that ourselves fairly soon, but I think you've saved us some trouble. I've been thinking of the Paulings only in terms of the breakup of their marriage. Since we began to think that at least one of the deaths in that room might not have been the work of Colin, who was the likeliest victim? And I was inclined to think Margot Pauling and that possibly her husband was the murderer, with the simple motive of revenge for her having left him. But if she and her husband were in contact with Greer and know how his deliveries to them had been come by, perhaps Greer himself had a motive for wanting her dead. If she threatened him, perhaps, after getting here. Even tried to blackmail him."

She shook her head. "I still can't make sense of it. I suppose Mr. Pauling could have come here after we separated in the village and got here in time to murder his wife before I got back. And I suppose Mr. Greer could have come here any time while I was out shopping and shot Mrs. Pauling. But how could either of them have known that there'd be a gun available? How could they have known about that leaf in the forest or that corpse on the battlefield? How could they have known that there'd be a possibility of leaving a body among a few other bodies so that Colin would be blamed? They couldn't have known it, could they?"

"No," he agreed, "they couldn't. So whoever came here came without any intention of committing a murder. They came for some other reason. Then, seeing Colin with a gun, shooting his grandparents, then himself, they couldn't resist the opportunity it gave of shooting Margot Pauling and adding her body to the slaughter."

"But he was seen by Jennifer Hyland and so had to dispose of her too."

"That's how it looks."

"You said she was struck on the head before she was drowned. Do you know what she was struck with?"

"Not for sure. There are men out hunting around the place where she was found to see if they can find a weapon. But there's one thing I can tell you about that. We noticed something unusual in the drawing-room here yesterday: the set of fire irons in the fireplace isn't complete. There are a shovel and a pair of tongs, but no poker. The blows on her head could have been inflicted by a poker."

Constance found herself doing something that she had been trying to avoid for the last twenty-four hours. It was visualising the scene in the drawing-room as it had been when she had walked in the morning before. She realised now that she had had hardly more than a glimpse of it. She had run from the room so quickly that she found it difficult to be sure that her memory of it was accurate. It seemed to her that what she had seen had been so deeply impressed on her brain that she would never forget it, yet how could she be certain of that?

"If you're right," she said slowly, picking her words, "then Margot Pauling wasn't in the room when Colin shot his grandparents. If she had been, she'd have been his first target, wouldn't she?"

"That seems likely for more than one reason," Frayne agreed.

"For more than one?"

"Yes, there's the obvious one that she'd have been what you called his first target because he probably hated her more than anybody, except perhaps his stepfather. His hatred for his grandparents appears to have been because of all the lies they'd told him about his mother, but she was the one who'd abandoned him and had no love for him. But there's some other evidence that she was on the terrace when Colin began his shooting. There's an ashtray on the table there with two or three cigarette stubs in it and the remains of a cigarette that had burnt itself out, only half-smoked. What it looks like is that she was sitting out there smoking when Colin began his murders; then, when she heard the shots, she dropped her cigarette in the ashtray and came running into the room to see what was happening and got shot herself."

"But not by Colin?"

"Really we aren't sure. There are only his fingerprints on the gun, and it was in just the place where it would have fallen from his hand beside him when he'd shot himself. If I could think of any reason why Jennifer Hyland should be murdered except that she'd seen something that was very dangerous to someone, I'd feel inclined to think that Colin was responsible for all the other murders."

A sense of acute tension made Constance suddenly restless, and getting up, she went to the window and stood looking out at the terrace. That was where Colin had loved to play chess and where today he ought to have been proudly setting up his chessmen and inducing Conrad Greer to play with him. Conrad Greer, who had almost certainly acquired the chessmen knowing them to have been stolen and who perhaps had shot the woman who had borne his son. If Colin had known only half of it, it would not have been astonishing that he should have gone berserk.

The terrace was where Margot Pauling had been sitting when she had heard the shooting begin. And she had dashed in to see what was happening instead of removing herself immediately to safety. A brave woman, even if there was not much else to be said in her favour.

"You know, you still haven't really told me why you wanted to see me this morning," Constance said. "You said it was partly to talk about the matter in general, but wasn't there some other reason too?"

"Well, I wanted to ask you about that poker," he said. "You've been in and out of that room a number of times since you first came here, I suppose. Did you ever notice if there was a poker as well as a shovel and tongs?"

She turned and went back to her chair at the table.

"No, I didn't," she said. "At this time of year you don't think about fires. I saw that there was a fire laid on the hearth so that they could light it if it got chilly in the evening, but I didn't notice the fire irons."

"So if they didn't have a poker there before all this happened, we've got to look for some other weapon," Frayne said.

"But if the poker was the weapon, it means Jennifer was attacked in this house."

"I think so, yes."

"And then carried to her car and driven away. Wouldn't that have needed a good deal of strength?"

"Yes, I should say a fair amount."

"I wish I knew what you really think about it all."

"So do I." He stood up. "It might help. Are you going home now?"

"I don't think so," she answered. "My daughter's coming down, as I understand it to give me some moral support. She'll be coming here, so I'll wait at least until she gets here."

"You've a family, have you?"

"A son and a daughter. My son's farming in New Zealand; my daughter . . . well, she lives in London."

"And you take on this kind of job quite frequently?"

"Not exactly this kind, as it's turned out."

"No, of course not. But you must run into some pretty strange situations sometimes, all the same."

"Fewer than you'd think. Most people are abysmally normal, or at least put up a show of being so as long as I'm around. *Pas devant les domestiques,* you know."

"Ah," he said, "I suppose I know what that means. Tell me, would you say that Jennifer Hyland was one of the normal, abysmal or otherwise?"

She stood up too, and together they moved towards the door.

"Now why should you ask me that?" she said.

"Only that we just could have been thinking about the whole thing the wrong way up. Suppose it was she who committed all the murders after delivering the birthday cake and was killed by someone who saw her do it. I can see certain arguments against that. How did she know there was a gun in the house? How did she know where it was kept? How did she lay her hands on it? And why might she have done it? Why? You've been living here in the house for a few days. Can you think of any reason why Jennifer Hyland might have wanted to exterminate the family?"

"So that's what you really came to ask me?" Constance said.

They had reached the closed front door and now stood still before it. Constance's hand was on the latch, but she did not turn it.

"Well, can you?" he asked.

"I can't think of anyone who'd have wanted to do that," she said.

"Can you think of any single one of them she might have wanted to kill? Margot Pauling, for instance?"

"Because . . ." She paused, trying to think of the implications of this new approach. "Because, say, she was in love with Conrad Greer and was afraid that Margot might take him away from her? And he saw her do it and killed her in fury at what she'd done?"

"Have you seen any sign that she and Greer had any interest in one another?"

"I've never even seen them together."

"Ah well," he said, sounding reluctant to give up a theory that had attracted him. "I'll have to stick to it that Colin killed his grandparents, but Jennifer must have seen something, you know, so it seems to me most probable that that was the shooting of Margot. Thank you for listening to me. I still need that formal statement from you. If you'll come into the police station later in the day, we'll settle that."

Constance opened the door for him and he went out.

As she closed the door behind him, she said aloud, her voice sounding strange and echoing in the empty house, "He can't have meant that. He can't have thought Jennifer killed off the family. He didn't. So what did he mean? The man isn't a fool."

It was at nearly half past twelve that Irene arrived at the house. A taxi brought her. She got out of it with a suitcase and a large, curiously shaped object, the nature of which Constance could not guess at. She saw Irene and the taxi from the window of her bedroom, to which she had returned to finish her small amount of packing. Irene put her finger on the door bell and left it there until, Constance presumed, she heard footsteps on the staircase and knew that someone was coming to let her in. Giving up the ringing then, Irene was standing with the suitcase in one hand and the unidentified object in the other, ready to enter.

She came in, put both things down in the hall, and kissed Constance.

"You look all right," Irene said in a faintly reproving tone, as if there were something improper about her mother looking all right after what she had been through. "I always forget how tough people like you can be. It's astonishing when you come to think of it. I mean, when you've led such a sheltered life and had so little experience. But I'm so glad you've survived so well."

Irene was a tall girl, slender and well proportioned, with chestnut hair to her shoulders and big greenish eyes. Her features were delicate, her skin pale and clear.

Whenever Constance met her after a fairly long interval she was always taken by surprise at how very good-looking Irene was.

Normally she did nothing to encourage such a view of her. Her usual dress was jeans and a T-shirt; she never wore make-up and never dreamed of having her really beautiful hair attended to by a hairdresser. Today, however, she was in a pretty pale-grey dress, subdued but, for her, amazingly elegant, was wearing long gold earrings, and had a slightly excessive amount of make-up around her eyes, which made them look very large and brilliant. Constance wondered if this might all be in honour of murder. Was it Irene's idea of the formality due on such an unusual and important occasion?

"Whatever is that?" Constance asked, pointing to the object that Irene had put down beside her suitcase. It was the case of a musical instrument, Constance had recognised, but of what kind she could not guess.

"It's a French horn," Irene answered. "I've just taken it up."

"What made you do that?"

"Well, someone told me it's the most difficult instrument to play that there is," Irene answered, "and I thought that was a challenge."

"Doesn't it interfere with your chanting?"

"I've given that up. I wasn't getting anywhere with it."

"So you won't be wanting to do any while you're here. That's a relief. But are you still living in that community?"

"No, I've moved out. I've got a flat of my own now. I told you I'd got a job, didn't I? It's in a bookshop. I'm rather enjoying it." Irene said this with a kind of surprise, as if the idea of enjoying a job were something astonishing.

"But then how did you get my letter?" Constance asked. "I addressed it to you at your old address."

"A friend of mine who sometimes calls in there brought it to me," Irene said. "Actually he's going to move into my flat later today. I left the keys with him. We're thinking of getting married."

"Now this is a bit too much of a good thing," Constance said. "You're looking all clean and tidy and as pretty as can be, you've got a job you like, and you're thinking of getting married. I can't believe it."

Irene put an arm round her and kissed her again.

"Take it easy, Mum," she said. "You know you're awfully pleased about it all."

"I admit the French horn somewhat reassures me," Constance said. "As long as you're doing something really absurd I feel you're still the girl I know."

"There's nothing absurd about a French horn," Irene said austerely.

"But there is about your taking it up. You've never been in the least musical."

"One can always develop, can't one? Perhaps I never had the right sort of encouragement. Look, have we got to stay out here in the hall? Can't we go and sit down somewhere and perhaps have a drink?"

"Come in here," Constance said and led the way to the dining-room. "I've been drinking more than really agrees with me. I only stayed here last night because I was feeling a bit drunk and was afraid of driving. What would you like?"

"What I really like is damson gin," Irene said. "There's a chap in the community who makes it. It's fabulous. But I don't suppose you've got any."

"No, I'm afraid you'll have to choose between sherry, gin, whisky, and brandy."

"Then sherry, please." Irene had sat down and was

looking round. "Mum, I like this house. It's just the
kind of house I hope I'll be able to afford some day. Do
you think people are going to be afraid of it because of
the murders that happened here?"

Constance was pouring out sherry for Irene and herself. "Are you hoping that that might bring the price
down to something within your reach?"

"Now who's being absurd?" Irene said. "Why are you
being so bitchy to me, Mum?"

"I'm sorry, I'm sorry, I'm really sorry, darling." Constance dropped into a chair, facing Irene. "After all the
things that have been happening, I don't think I'm
quite myself. Tell me about this man you're thinking of
marrying."

"His name's Samuel. And he's teaching me to play
the French horn. And he's got a job with a small publishing firm who publish mostly very technical things
about archaeology. He's really very learned. I know
you'll like him. And he's fifty-two."

"But that's more than twenty years older than you!"
Constance exclaimed.

"What's wrong with that. He's very youthful in his
outlook, and I think I'm rather mature in mine."

This was something that Constance had never noticed, but she did not dispute it.

"You may be right," she said, falling back on her
usual formula for avoiding an argument. "Has he any
name besides Samuel?"

"Yes, it's Blythe. And I think that's a very nice name,
because he's really such a blithe person."

"I'm glad you like it. My trouble is I can't get used to
this habit that's got around of calling people by their
first names, and probably kissing them too, the first
time you meet them. It's my generation." Constance
had begun to think that marrying someone twenty

years older than herself might be just what Irene needed. "Am I going to meet him?"

"Of course. I'd have brought him down here today if he hadn't been getting settled into my flat."

"How long are you staying?"

"That rather depends on how long you need me. They've been very understanding at the shop. Naturally there was no problem about my coming today, as it's Sunday, but when I phoned my boss this morning to tell him what had happened, he told me I needn't hurry back. He just wants me to phone him this evening to tell him what the position is."

So that he could question Irene closely, get an inside story about the murders, and write it up quickly to sell to some newspaper, Constance thought. Then she began to wonder what was happening to her. Why was she having such shocking thoughts about everybody? Had she always been like that, she wondered. Had a sceptical attitude, a lack of sympathy, a tendency to mockery on her part really been to blame for most of Irene's eccentricities? She was a dear girl, really. Had not the speed with which she had come to Long Meldon demonstrated that? Constance hoped very much that she was going to like Samuel.

The front door bell rang.

Irene jerked upright in her chair. "Who's that? Is it the police?

"I should think that's unlikely," Constance said. "They've been here already this morning."

She went to the front door and opened it. Pauling stood there.

"I'm glad you're still here," he said. "I wasn't sure you would be."

"I'm leaving soon," she said. "But come in." He

stepped inside, and she closed the door. "Have the police been to see you this morning?"

"Yes, that's why I came," he said. "I wanted to find out if you can make any more sense of things than I can. After all, we were together for some of yesterday morning, weren't we? Have you told them that?"

"Oh yes." She was leading him towards the dining-room. "This is my daughter, Irene; this is Mr. Pauling, the husband of Margot, who was shot by Colin."

"Hallo," Irene said rather lugubriously. His arrival did not seem to exhilarate her.

"Hallo," Pauling replied in an equally muted tone.

After that there was a silence. Then Constance remembered to offer Pauling a drink, and he asked for whisky. But though he had appeared ready, indeed eager, to talk when he first saw Constance, the presence of Irene seemed to have discouraged him. He looked as if he did not know what he was doing there.

"Irene got here only a few minutes ago," Constance said, feeling that the two must be explained to one another. "She heard about the shooting on the seven o'clock news and she knew that I was working here, so she came straight down. But she doesn't really know much about what's happened."

"Does she know about this unfortunate girl, Jennifer?" Pauling asked.

"Come to think of it, I don't suppose she does," Constance said. "Irene, there seems to have been a murder that the press haven't got hold of yet. A girl called Jennifer Hyland, who's been running a café in the village for some time, made a cake for Colin's birthday, which should have been today, and she brought it up here yesterday morning and left it on the kitchen table. And then she disappeared. Her sister got very worried about her not coming home and got in touch with the police about it, and this morning they found the girl drowned in a pool near here. Only before drowning she'd been hit hard on the head with what the police are inclined to think may have been the poker from the drawing-room fireplace here. In other words, she was probably knocked unconscious here and carried out to her car and driven up to this pool where they found her, all because she saw something which was very dangerous to somebody."

"So you mean Colin didn't murder all those people?" Irene said.

"Perhaps not all," Constance answered. "What I thought Inspector Frayne believed was that someone came in and found what Colin had done or was just doing, and as there was a gun lying there handy, he decided to grab it and add another death to the count. And Jennifer saw that and so was killed and taken away and dumped in the pool."

"And that's absurd, you know," Pauling said. "It doesn't take one very serious thing into account."

Constance turned her head to look at him question-ingly. He did not meet her gaze because he was looking intently at Irene, who was returning his stare with an expression of uncertainty, which was not characteristic of her. She usually knew what she thought on most matters.

"Why is it absurd?" Constance asked.

"Because whoever did it had to get away from the pool, as well as to it," Pauling said. "All right, suppose Jennifer walked in on the scene here and saw someone take the gun that had fallen out of Colin's hand and shoot someone with it—Margot, the police are obvi-ously fairly sure—and suppose Jennifer made a scene, even tried to stop it, perhaps tried to ring 999, and so was hit on the head and knocked unconscious, then bundled into her own car, driven up to the pool, and pushed into it—then whoever did that had to get away. And he had to walk. If he'd driven Jennifer to the pool in her car, as I understand he did, he can't have driven away from there in his own. So he had to walk back into Long Meldon, if that was where he came from, and take up his normal life as if he'd never been away. And that would have taken a bit of doing. So in my view the police idea is absurd. I think the girl gave some hitch-hiker a lift in the lane, and when he'd murdered her, he simply walked on along it, I don't know in which direction, and by now he's God knows where."

"Tell me," Irene said, still eyeing him in her unusually dubious way, "have you ever been in Long Meldon before?"

"Not for around fifteen or sixteen years," he answered. "I live in Sydney."

"Ah, but you have been here long ago," she said.

"I think so, yes. I'm fairly sure of it, though I can't remember much about it. I used to live in Bracklington and I'd a liking for walking in those days and I probably came here sometime on one of my rambles, though I've an impression it's all very much changed. I don't seem to recognize any of it."

"But the pool wouldn't have changed, would it?"

"Perhaps not. No, I imagine it wouldn't. Why?"

"Only that if you'd never been here before, I mean literally never, you couldn't possibly have known there was any pool where there is one. I know it, you know. I used to live in Bracklington myself and I did a bit of rambling too, and I remember once some friends and I sat down by that pool and ate our lunches there."

A look of astonished anger appeared on Pauling's face.

"You're implying I could have been the person who took the girl up to it and drowned her!" he exclaimed.

"No," Irene said mildly, "I was trying to clear you. I thought if you didn't know these parts at all, you couldn't possibly know where to find a pool to drown her in. But you did know about it, so I can't help you—that's all I meant."

"Only how did I get back to the Green Dragon without being noticed?" There was a mocking look on his face now, as if he had decided that she need not be taken seriously. "I still believe in the hitch-hiker."

"Perhaps someone did notice you," Irene said. "You can't yet be sure they didn't, can you?"

"No doubt the police will find out about that fairly soon. I'll either be under arrest by the evening or else on my way back to Sydney. But if you don't like my theory about the hitch-hiker . . ." He paused.

"Yes?" Constance said.

He looked back at her. His anger seemed only to have been momentary. His face now was sad and tired.

"No," he said, "think it out for yourself. Logically there's really only one person who could have done it. I mean, who could have got away from the pool without being noticed. But I'm not going to start making trouble when, after all, I could be wrong. Mrs. Lawley, to go back to what I said when I came here, you and I had coffee together yesterday morning and we saw Jennifer Hyland leaving in her car, you thought to bring the birthday cake here. But the police seem to be sure she didn't come here straight away and want to know where she spent the short time they can't account for. Have you any ideas about it?"

She shook her head. "None at all. My guess is, it isn't important. But I think I understand what you mean when you say there's only one person who could have

got away from the pool without any risk of being noticed. You mean Conrad Greer, don't you? I believe the
pool is only a little way up the lane beyond his house.
So all he had to do, if he killed Jennifer, was walk
straight home. He might have had bad luck and been
seen by someone in the lane, but I've noticed that very
few people come along it, on foot or by car. And if your
wife was his victim, he had a possible motive for getting
rid of her, hadn't he?"

"For getting rid of Margot? *He* had?" But though his
tone was incredulous, it seemed to Constance that his
eyes were wary. "You don't mean because she broke off
with him all those years ago."

"I wasn't actually thinking of that," she said.

"And you don't mean he may have got the idea that
she was going to take Colin away from him. If anyone
thought that, they didn't know Margot. The last thing
she ever wanted was to be burdened with a child."

"Let's leave it at that," she said. "As you said yourself
just now, I could be wrong, and I don't want to start
making trouble for an innocent person."

"So you're very sure of yourself, aren't you, but for
some reason you're afraid of saying so?" His tone had
suddenly become hostile. "Then we'll none of us say
what we think. I'd better be going. Goodbye. Goodbye,
Irene."

She did not answer, but sat looking thoughtfully after him as Constance saw him to the front door.

When she came back, Irene said, "Of course you realise he's the murderer, don't you?"

"What on earth makes you say that?" Constance
asked.

"Oh, it's just something one knows," Irene said. "I
knew it as soon as I saw him. You've always known I
was very intuitive, haven't you? And during this last

year or two in the community, I've been specially train-
ing myself. I could tell at once. Besides that, you're
afraid of him."

This was a little nearer to the truth than Constance
had expected. In the last few minutes, without understanding it, she had felt a sense of fear of the man building up in her. Doing her best to rationalise it, she said,
"There's a possibility that he and Conrad Greer were
involved together in something pretty crooked. And if
they were and Margot knew about it, or was even involved in it herself, and if she threatened Greer after
she got home that she might be going to give him away
if he didn't pay her blackmail, then he would have had
a motive for killing her. But that applies to Pauling too
—only, as he pointed out, it's unlikely he could have
got all the way back to the Green Dragon from the pool
without anyone noticing him, whereas Greer had only a
short walk back to his house."

"Mum, darling, you really are too simple," Irene said
and, as Constance sat down again at the table, reached
out and patted her hand affectionately. "You're saying
precisely what he wanted you to say. It's why he came
here. It was to put that idea into your head so that
you'd suggest it to the police, instead of his having to
do it himself. It would be ever so much more subtle and
convincing coming from you than from him. But the
obvious fact is he simply walked back into the village
after leaving the poor girl in the pool and just had the
sort of good luck that people like him often have of not
meeting anybody. If he had met somebody, he'd probably have said what a nice day it was and what a pleasant
walk he'd been having. But he knew he hadn't met anybody, so he knew he was quite safe to say what he did
to you. But what's this crooked thing he and Conrad

Greer are supposed to have been involved in and that it
frightened you to mention to him?"

Constance did not answer at once. She had not made
up her mind how far to confide in Irene. Then she said
uncertainly, "For all I know, there may be no truth in it
whatever. That's why I didn't want to talk about it. But
the police seem to think that Conrad Greer's been a
receiver of stolen property for some time and his shop
in Bracklington is just a front for his other activities.
They've been keeping an eye on him recently, and it
seems he's been shipping stuff off to the Paulings in
Australia, though whether or not they knew it was
stolen isn't quite clear. I think they did, but I don't
think it's certain, any more than it's absolutely sure
that Greer's really a fence. He had some stolen chessmen in his possession yesterday, but he may not have
known they were stolen. He was going to give them as a
birthday present to Colin, because chess was the stron-
gest passion in his life, and Greer brought them here a
few hours after the murders and Inspector Frayne found
them and pounced on them and took them away. And
apparently it's definite that they were stolen, but if
Greer had known that, would he have brought them
here when the place was crawling with police?"

"Of course he would have," Irene said. "If you've a
certain sort of criminal mind, you believe you can get
away with anything. Or he might actually have brought
them here on purpose to induce you to think just what
you do—that he'd never have taken the risk of bringing
them if he'd known they were stolen. Again, it'll be
much more subtle and convincing if it's you who suggests that to the police than if he has to do it. Oh, Mum
dear, it's really time I came down to look after you, isn't
it? You've got such a nice innocent mind. Meanwhile,
d'you know what I'd like?"

"Some lunch?"

"Oh yes, some lunch, of course. But I'd very much like to meet this Conrad Greer. I remember his shop in Bracklington, but I've never been into it. Could we get him here on some pretext or other? Or could we call on him?"

The thought of getting lunch was comforting to Constance. It was normal, it was rational, it was something that she knew how to do. She finished her sherry and stood up.

"Are you beginning to have doubts about your instant diagnosis of Kenneth Pauling as a murderer?" she asked.

"Good Lord, no, that's as clear as day," Irene answered. "But I'm very interested in the criminal mind. In people, I mean, who truly reject the dictates of society. I'd really like to meet Conrad Greer."

Seven

Constance did not want to meet Conrad Greer. She did not want to meet anybody. She wished she were at home, sitting down by herself to eat a ham sandwich or perhaps some beans on toast, with no one, not even Irene, to intrude on her peaceful privacy. But Irene was here and ready to eat some lunch even if after it she would be anxious to proceed with some detective work. For that was what it was, Constance thought, that Irene really wanted to do. She might have claimed that by sheer instinct she had already spotted the murderer, but it would please her, would make her feel that she was pandering successfully to the prejudices of people more commonplace than herself, if she could collect some evidence against him.

Meanwhile, there was lunch. Thank heaven for lunch, Constance thought. Shopping in the village the day before, she had bought some garlic paté, which was in the refrigerator. Putting it out on plates for Irene and herself, she made some toast and some coffee, then called to Irene to come and eat in the kitchen. Irene strolled in, looking deeply abstracted, lost in thoughts which no doubt she felt that this was not the right time to express. She settled down to spreading paté on her toast, either munching dreamily or gazing out of the window.

She had finished toast and paté and was leaning her elbows on the table, holding her cup of coffee in both hands, when she said, "All right, you don't want us to call on Greer, but what do you want to do? Are we going to stay here till they've solved the crime?"

"You needn't stay at all, you know," Constance said. "It was your idea to come."

"And a good thing I did, as I said. You'll swallow anything anyone tells you without even trying to see what's behind it. That's as long as it isn't me that tells you. You never believe anything I say."

"Oh, it surely isn't as bad as that," Constance said. "You aren't a liar; it's just that you let your fantasies run away with you."

"You mean I con myself before I start trying to con other people."

"That's a rather unkind way of putting it."

"But it's what you think."

Constance was a little surprised that Irene should have gone so far in self-analysis. She began to wonder what sort of man Samuel was. Had his influence had something to do with it?

"It's just that what I've got to do this afternoon is to go to the police station in Bracklington and make a full statement about finding the bodies and so on," she said. "You can come with me or not, as you like."

"And after that you mean to go home?"

"It's what I'd like to do unless there's some very good reason for staying here."

"Very well, let's go home. You've had a bad time here. I can understand you want to get away. But perhaps we could look in on Greer in the morning. I mean, he'll be back in his shop, won't he? We could go in and perhaps even buy something, a pretty snuff-box or something. We could tell him I'm getting married and that you're looking for a wedding present for me; then our going in wouldn't look suspicious."

"I can't think of anything that would look more suspicious," Constance said. "If you really want to go in to see him, we'll tell him we want to talk to him about the murders and find out what he thinks. That strikes me as a fairly normal thing to do."

"All right, if that's how you want to handle it. Now what about getting along to that police station you've got to go to?"

Constance stood up and automatically started to put the plates and cups that they had used into the dishwasher when she realised that she would not be here to run it later, so she washed them under the tap and was in the act of putting them away in the cupboard from which she had taken them when the door bell rang yet again.

"That'll be the police this time, won't it?" Irene said.

"I don't know," Constance replied.

"Are you expecting anyone else?"

"No."

"Well, you won't tell them what I said about the Pauling man, will you? That's something just between you and me."

"I wouldn't dream of it."

"It would be all right if we had some of the sort of evidence that would convince people like them, but I

know how they can sneer and try to make you feel a
fool if they don't understand you."

The bell rang again. Constance hurried out into the
hall and opened the door.

A man whom she had never seen before stood there.
He was a small man in a neat grey suit and a grey-and-
white-striped shirt with a sober, dark blue tie. He was
about forty, had a long, smooth-featured face and sandy
hair neatly parted on one side and a smile that looked
politely diffident but did not reach his small grey eyes,
which regarded Constance with what struck her as a
coolly observant manner. She wondered for a moment
if he was a plain-clothes detective, but thought that he
was too small ever to have been accepted into the police
force.

"Mrs. Lawley?" he asked.

"Yes," she said.

"I believe you're the caretaker here."

"The housekeeper. And I'm leaving shortly."

"Ah, I'm sorry I got it wrong," he said. "I must have
misunderstood Mr. Frayne. My name is Collis." He
brought a card out of his pocket and handed it to her. "I
belong to the firm of Stevenson, Bartholomew and Collis. We've acted for some time as Colonel Barrow's solicitors. Mr. Frayne chased me down in my home. Being
Sunday, no one was in the office, but he was very anxious that one of us should come out here immediately
to catch you before you left so that we could make
arrangements for a valuer to come in—probate, you
know—and for me to take possession of any obvious
valuables such as jewellery, silver, and so on, to put
them in our strong-room. Naturally you'll want to ver-
ify my credentials, so please ring up Mr. Frayne and ask
him if I'm to be trusted."

He had spoken rapidly and earnestly, but ended with

a sudden little nervous explosion of laughter, as if there were something very amusing to him about the idea that anyone could doubt the integrity of a member of the firm of Stevenson, Bartholomew and Collis.

The name was familiar to Constance as that of one of the leading firms of solicitors in Bracklington. The only matter in doubt was whether this man was indeed their Mr. Collis.

"I think I ought to do that," she said.

"Please do, please do. Only proper. I would be much happier if you'd do that."

He laughed again, and glad to contribute to his happiness, Constance picked up the telephone and dialled the police station in Bracklington.

While she was speaking to Inspector Frayne and being told that Mr. Mortimer Collis was to be expected to call on her that afternoon and that he was entirely to be trusted, the man stayed outside on the doorstep, as if to make it clear that he was not the kind of man who might rush in, slam the door behind him, and do damage of some kind to a defenceless woman. When she had put the telephone down again, she invited him to come in. Irene, meanwhile, had come to the doorway of the kitchen to find out what was going on, and Constance introduced her and the man to one another. Then she took him into the dining-room and Irene followed.

"This is without doubt the most shocking event in my experience," he said as they all sat down at the table, "and I have been with the firm for nearly twenty years. Of course, I never was happy about that poor boy. I call him a poor boy although I suppose he was really a young monster. But it wasn't his fault. I can't persuade myself it was really his fault. If he had been born without the normal complement of arms and legs, we'd all be sorry for him, but what he was born without was a moral sense, and we can't forgive that."

Irene murmured, "The fault, dear Brutus, is not in our stars, but in our genes."

"I beg your pardon?" he said.

"Nothing," she said. "All the same, if you haven't got arms and legs, you can't start killing people, even if you'd like to. But basically I'm sure you're right; he was a poor boy. I'm very sorry for him."

"If he'd lived," Constance said, "who would have taken care of him?"

"I'm not sure," the man answered. "It would have been primarily a case for the police."

"No, I meant if none of the tragedy had happened," she said. "The Barrows were both around eighty. Probably neither of them would have lived much longer, or even if they had, they wouldn't have been capable of looking after a very difficult adolescent. Do you know if they'd made any provision for that?"

"As a matter of fact, I do, but . . ." He paused, evidently considering whether or not this was something too confidential for him to talk about. "Well, I don't see why I shouldn't tell you, if you're interested," he went on. "I've told the police. Colonel Barrow had made provision for the eventuality you mentioned. My firm were to be responsible for the boy. Mr. Stevenson, our senior partner, was to be his guardian."

"But they'd provided for him, had they?" Irene said. "I mean, they'd left their money to him."

Constance felt that the question should not have been asked. She assumed that the contents of the Barrows' wills was confidential, at least for the moment. After their funerals, perhaps, or after the inquests, it would become a matter of public knowledge, but at present this small, precise man would have no right to

disclose it. She did not know that lawyers often take
the obligation of confidentiality somewhat less seriously than is expected of them.

"It happens to be a rather interesting case," he said.
"The Barrows left all they possessed to their grandson.
But in the event of his predeceasing them, then their
estate was to pass to their daughter, Mrs. Pauling. And
at the moment, you see, there seems to be some degree
of uncertainty which died first, the mother or the son.
If he shot his mother, as it was at first assumed he had,
then he, of course, survived her and stood to inherit the
Barrows' money. But if in fact he had killed himself
before someone else came in and killed Mrs. Pauling,
then she probably survived the boy and was their heir."

"But can you inherit money as the result of committing a crime?" Constance asked. "I thought you
couldn't."

"Ah, there's that to be considered, of course," the
solicitor said. "I'm not sure, however, what the position
is when the heir is a minor and mentally not entirely
responsible for his actions. It's a very interesting question. But in the end, in this case, it happens not to make
much difference. The boy himself, of course, had made
no will, so anything he might have inherited would
have passed to his next of kin, his mother, and she, we
believe, though this has yet to be confirmed, made a
will leaving all she had to her husband. So whether the
Barrow money came directly to her or only after it had
belonged briefly to her son, it will in any case end up in
the possession of Mr. Pauling. He happens, as perhaps
you know, to be in Long Meldon at the moment, which
is very convenient. There's the matter of tax to be considered, of course. It will come to a considerably larger
amount if it turns out that the boy was capable of inher-
iting his grandparents' estate, as there would be two lots

of death duties, but it may well be that it isn't possible. However, that brings me to what I really came for this afternoon. I hadn't realised that you intended to leave the house, Mrs. Lawley, and I wanted to arrange with you when it would be convenient for you to let Mr. Grigson, the valuer we usually employ on these occasions, to come and make an estimate of the contents of the house so that we can proceed with calculating the tax that will be due. And then there's the matter of removing any outstanding valuables to safekeeping in our strong-room. Perhaps you can help us there."

"I don't know anything about that," Constance said. "I'm sure you won't feel offended, but the fact is I don't like to feel responsible for removing anything, but perhaps you can get someone from the police to go round the house with you. And the same with your Mr. Grigson. My daughter and I are leaving for our home in Bracklington this afternoon, but the police, of course, have keys to the house and could show him round."

"Ah yes, that will plainly be best." Mr. Collis stood up. "I'll explain the situation to them, and no doubt we can arrange something. Meanwhile, thank you for your time. I'll say good-day."

It was Irene who saw him to the door. Coming back after a moment, she gave a cheerful giggle.

"Poor little man, you offended him terribly, suspecting him of being a thief," she said. "I don't suppose anything of the sort has ever happened to a member of the firm of Stevenson, Bartholomew and Collis. You should have seen how stiffly he walked to his car, pretending he didn't feel like hitting me."

"But I didn't suspect him of anything," Constance said. "I'm sure he's just what he said he was."

"But he didn't think you did."

"Well, I'm sorry. I'm sure he's just as respectable as

he looks, but I could hardly let someone I'd never met before walk off with Mrs. Barrow's jewellery, if she has any. I don't know anything about that. Now I suppose we'll have to wait till Mr. Collis comes back with a policeman. I do see that valuables shouldn't be left lying around in an empty house."

"It's interesting, isn't it, that Pauling's going to inherit everything from the Barrows?" Irene said. "I knew he was the murderer of his wife, but I thought it was out of rage at her leaving him. It hadn't occurred to me he'd a good solid financial motive as well.

"He told me about that motive himself," Constance said. "I don't think it has anything to do with the murders."

"And why did he tell you about the motive? Wasn't it simply to seem to be awfully straightforward and honest to lull your suspicions? Darling, you are so easy to fool. But have we really got to wait for the police now?"

"I think we'd better."

As it turned out, they did not have to wait very long. In less than an hour Mr. Collis returned, accompanied, to Constance's surprise, by three constables. It seemed an unnecessarily large force to send for the protection of the Barrows' silver and jewellery. But only one of these policemen remained in the house with the solicitor, going from room to room, opening doors and cupboards, and from time to time extracting some object which apparently they considered valuable. The other two men remained in the garden, poking about amongst flowers and shrubs, appearing to be searching for something.

Irene seemed to have been right that Constance had offended Mr. Collis, for he was far less friendly now than he had been during his first visit. But she and Irene did not stay to see his work completed. Constance at

last finished packing her suitcase, Irene collected her
own case and her French horn, and the two of them set
off for Bracklington in the Mini.

Constance felt a sense of intense relief when they left
Long Meldon behind them. Not only Riverside, but the
whole village, seemed pervaded with horror. Passing
Jenny's Café she saw that curtains were drawn across
the windows and that a notice hung on the door, saying
CLOSED. They passed the Green Dragon, where she supposed Kenneth Pauling was still staying. It was unlikely
that he would leave before his wife's funeral, at the
earliest, and if in fact he stood to inherit all that the
Barrows had had to leave, then he would probably want
a chance to consult their solicitors before leaving for
Australia. If he was able to leave. Might he not have to
stay here? For the first time since Irene had proclaimed
her certainty of his guilt, Constance found herself wondering if her daughter might not have more wisdom
than she had ever given her credit for.

The afternoon was bright, the sunshine glittering on
the road ahead of them and on the vivid green of meadows to left and right of it. When they drove into Bracklington, Constance drove first to the police station.
There she asked for Inspector Frayne, but it was the
monosyllabic Sergeant Randall, who had accompanied
Frayne on his first visit to Riverside, who took her statement, gave it to her to sign, thanked her, and would
have ushered them out to the car if Irene had not
checked him with a question.

"Those men who are out at Riverside with Mr. Collis,
sergeant," she said, "I suppose they're looking for the
weapon that was used to brain Jennifer Hyland, aren't
they?"

He had one of the blankest faces that Constance had

ever seen. It showed no trace of expression as he answered, "I couldn't say, Miss Lawley."

"But of course you could," Irene said. "It's just that
you think you shouldn't."

"Come along, Irene," Constance said. "We don't
want to waste the sergeant's time."

"Only I can't see why he shouldn't tell us that,"
Irene said. "They're looking for that poker, aren't they,
sergeant?"

He merely gazed at her without making any answer at
all, while Constance, grasping Irene by the arm, suc-
ceeded in steering her out to the Mini.

They spent the evening watching television, except
for a short interval when Irene telephoned Samuel. She
did it while Constance was cooking a meal for them, or
rather, heating up a steak-and-kidney pie from Marks &
Spencer that she had in the freezer and boiling some
potatoes and some frozen spinach to go with it. Living
alone, as she had been doing for the last few years, she
had grown to rely more and more on take-away foods,
which she need not trouble to cook for herself. But
oddly enough, one of the attractions of the kind of job
to which she was sent by the Bracklington Helpers was
that it made demands on her culinary abilities. The
kind of people for whom she worked naturally expected
her to provide good food for them, and she always felt
more pleasure in cooking with care and interest and
being praised for it than she would ever have expected
of herself in the days when she had cooked for a family
and sometimes felt very tired of it.

She went to bed early, far more tired than she normally was when she returned home from a job, and was
asleep before Irene went to her room.

In the morning Constance was wakened by a strange
sound. At first it seemed to her to be part of a dream in

which she was still lost, and burying her head in her pillow, she tried to emerge from her drowsiness and to escape from the noise. But it was not a dream. It was Irene, practising the French horn. The fact penetrated suddenly to Constance's consciousness and she recognized abruptly that in fact she was wide awake.

She sat up in bed. Until now she had been congratulating herself on the fact that Irene had given up her chanting and so the sound of it would not be inflicted on her, but this was more penetrating, more overpowering than the chanting had ever been. She wondered if Samuel really believed that Irene could be taught to play the thing properly or whether, once they were married, he would bring her round tactfully to recognizing that music was not her strong point and that something quiet, like painting water-colours, might be a more rewarding form of self-expression for her.

Getting up and putting on her dressing-gown, Constance went to the door of Irene's room, put her head into it, and shouted, "Breakfast in ten minutes!"

She was not sure if Irene heard her, but she went downstairs and proceeded to make coffee and toast.

She had reached her second cup of coffee when Irene appeared, also in a dressing-gown, and sitting down at the kitchen table, where Constance ate most of her meals when she was at home, helped herself to coffee and toast and marmalade.

"I've been thinking," Irene announced. It was an activity for which Constance had often felt her daughter was not too well fitted, but she waited for her to go on. "We agreed yesterday, didn't we, that we'd look in on the Greer shop this morning?"

"I suppose we did," Constance said reluctantly.

"You don't want to do it now?" Irene asked.

"Not particularly. I'd like to have a very quiet day

and, among other things, ring the Helpers and find out if I am going to be paid anything for the time I put in at Long Meldon. I was taken on for a week, but I only stayed four days and they were a bit peculiar, so perhaps I ought not to expect to be paid at all."

"Now that's just like you!" Irene exclaimed. "Of course they must pay you for the whole week. It wasn't your fault that things got peculiar."

"I certainly hope not."

"Have you a contract of employment? Have you a clause written into it that in the event of circumstances beyond your control you have to return home early, you have to forfeit any of the amount that would normally have been due to you for doing the full time?"

"Good heavens, no! It's never anything as formal as that. Mrs. Jay at the Helpers rings me up and asks me if I'm free to take on a job, and she tells me a little about it and I get in my car and tootle along to it. But what's happened to you, Irene? You always said one shouldn't think about money. You disdained it."

"Well, I've changed, that's all," Irene said. "I like it."

"I'm so glad to hear it. Not that one should think too much about it if one's fortunate enough not to be compelled to do so, but I think it's a healthy sign to take a reasonable interest in it."

"Mum, you aren't *short* of money, are you?" Irene asked. "I mean, you take on the sort of job you do because you want an interest in life, not because you couldn't get by financially without it? Because if that's how it is, I'm sure Samuel and I could help you."

Constance had never in her life expected to hear such words from Irene. She was beginning to feel that she had somehow badly misunderstood her daughter.

"That's very sweet of you and I do appreciate it," she said, "but you're quite right—I take on these jobs because normally I enjoy them, though of course the pay is welcome. I don't suppose I could have afforded to go to Madeira last year if I hadn't been earning. But I don't think your Samuel should have to finance my luxuries. I'm hoping he won't regard having a mother-in-law as a burden. But we were talking about going to the Greer shop this morning. I don't mind going if that's what you want to do, but are you sure it's wise?"

"Why shouldn't it be?"

"Only that we're bound to find ourselves getting more and more involved with these murders when it would obviously be best to leave them to the police."

"Why obviously?"

"Well, it's their job, isn't it? We'll only get under their feet."

"They always used to be supposed to have such big feet, didn't they? One doesn't seem to hear so much about that any more." Irene reached for a second slice of toast. "But I'd like to meet the man, you know. I'd like to be able to trust my own intuitions. Suppose when I meet him I feel quite certain that he's the murderer and that my certainty about Pauling was wrong; that would be very interesting scientifically. It isn't always one has the opportunity of making an experiment like that. But if you don't want to come, I could go by myself."

The thought of letting Irene loose in the Greer shop, making whatever form of experiment happened to appeal to her imagination, filled Constance with consternation. Hastily she said, "No, it's all right; I'll come. And, if you like, we'll look for a wedding present for you. You must tell me if you see something you like."

"Yesterday you said that would look very suspicious," Irene said. "You said we ought simply to talk straight away about the murders."

"Yes, it's what I think we ought to do, but if it's a case of really buying you a present, I don't see why we shouldn't do it, though I suppose when it comes to the point, I ought to supply you with sheets and towels, or perhaps cooking-pots or a dishwasher or something."

"Please, please!" Irene cried. "Let's look for something nice at Greer's. Samuel and I haven't the least idea how we mean to live. We might live in a caravan or somewhere there isn't any electricity or go prowling around Europe for a while on bicycles or even on foot. I'll tell you when we need the sheets and towels. But now let's go along to Greer's."

She stood up and started to clear the table.

They were both dressed and ready to leave for their visit to Conrad Greer's shop when they were checked by the arrival of a visitor.

For a moment Constance could not think who the woman was who stood on the doorstep, though she knew that she had seen her before. It was the scarf over her head that did it, nearly hiding her carefully arranged grey curls. She was a tall, sombre-faced woman of about fifty, and when Constance had seen her last, as she quickly remembered, she had been in trousers and a shirt, not in the neat light blue suit that she was wearing now. She was Mrs. Newcome, who had cleaned Riverside for the Barrows.

"Good morning, Mrs. Lawley," she said. "I hope I haven't come at an inconvenient time."

"Oh no, come in," Constance said, though she could not think why the woman should want to see her, unless it was simply to gossip about the tragedy at Riverside. She took her into the sitting-room and introduced her to Irene.

"Good morning," Mrs. Newcome said. "I'm glad to see you here. Your mother must need some support af-

ter what she's been through. Mrs. Lawley—" She
turned to Constance. "I'd be grateful for some advice,
but not if I'm intruding. The fact is, this morning was
one of my usual mornings for Riverside, but as I'm not
wanted there now, I thought I'd come into town and
have my hair done and do a bit of shopping, and then I
thought, well, perhaps Mrs. Lawley could tell me if I
ought to go to the police or if I'm worrying about nothing. I don't want to go to the police. Once you get
mixed up with them, you don't know where you may
end up, perhaps having to be a witness in a court or
something. But I want to do my duty."

They had all sat down in the small bright room that
overlooked a small garden in which there were still a
few roses in bloom, though they were past their summer prime and the September blooming had not yet
begun.

"I'm sure you do," Constance said, "though I'd be
surprised if there's anything useful in any advice I can
give you."

Mrs. Newcome clasped her hands around the bulging
plastic handbag that she was carrying.

"Some of it I've already told the police," she said.
"They came round asking questions, and they told me
they wanted to know if I'd seen Miss Hyland any time
on Saturday morning. Well, I had, as I told them. I saw
her just after she'd driven away from the café and I
waved to her and she came into my house and had a
cup of coffee with me. I don't know why, but the police
seemed very interested in that. She was only with me
about twenty minutes or thereabouts. I didn't see why
it should be important."

"I think I understand why it is," Constance said.
"They've been worried, you see, because they think she
was murdered only just before I got back to Riverside,

yet if she'd gone straight there after I saw her leave the café, she must have been in the house some time. And that upset all their ideas of how the murders happened. But if she spent some time with you, there's no problem about that."

"Those murders!" Mrs. Newcome said. "Well, I think I told you I'd seen him shriek and storm, didn't I, and that I was always very careful with him myself, but I never dreamt it would come to murder. Trouble of some sort wouldn't have surprised me, but murder! He could be a nice lad, too, in between whiles, so I sort of got attached to him. But I suppose finding out the truth about his mother was just too much for someone like him. I don't understand why he killed his grandparents, though. They'd been very good to him."

"He seems to have been furious with them because of the lies they'd told him," Constance said, "and I believe in his place I'd have been furious too. It would have been far better for him to have had to face the truth from the beginning."

"Trial by fury," Irene observed. "He tried them in his own mind for perjury and found them guilty."

"But it isn't about that cup of coffee you gave Miss Hyland that you want my advice, is it?" Constance said. "You say you've already told the police about that."

"No, it isn't about that," Mrs. Newcome said. "The trouble is, I think, I'm maybe just being silly, thinking about something that doesn't mean anything. If I'd thought of telling the police about it when they were in my house, it would have seemed natural, so to speak, and they might have been interested or they might not; it wouldn't have been my responsibility. But I don't want them thinking I'm the sort of person who pokes her nose into things just for the thrill of it. Honestly, I'm not like that, Mrs. Lawley."

"I'm sure you're not, Mrs. Newcome," Constance said.

"I did feel tempted to just ring them up and tell them the facts and ring off—you know what I mean, one of those anonymous phone calls one hears the police are always getting. But I knew I wouldn't respect myself if I did that. So then I thought I wouldn't do anything about it. But then I suddenly thought, as I was coming into Bracklington to get my hair done, I'd just look in on you and see if you think I ought to go to the police after all."

By now Constance was feeling that whatever the information was of which Mrs. Newcome was in possession it should most certainly be given to the police. The buildup that she had given it made it seem sure that it was important.

"Well, what's your problem?" Constance asked.

"It's just that I saw Mr. Greer in the village in the afternoon," Mrs. Newcome replied. She said it almost in a whisper, as if she were not sure that she wanted even Irene to overhear her. "He drove up to the café and went in, and in a minute he came out again. I saw him because I was just going into the grocer's. And when I came out the car was gone, but a funny thing was . . ." She hesitated, frowning as if she found some difficulty in following her own line of thought. "There's a card they hang on the door, saying OPEN or CLOSED, depending which way round they hang it. But I'm sure it said OPEN when I went into the grocer's, as it always was on a Saturday afternoon—that's when the best trade was—but when I came out, it said CLOSED."

"I see," Constance said. She did not exactly see, but she began to have a feeling that what she had been told might indeed be important. "We know now, of course, that Jennifer Hyland wasn't there to run things in the normal way, but isn't there a woman who works there, a small woman who wears a pink overall? If she was there, she could have kept things going, couldn't she?"

"Mrs. Crisp," Mrs. Newcome said. "She doesn't work on Saturday afternoon; she and her husband always come into town to do the weekend shopping. It's cheaper if you come in to the supermarket here than if you stick to the grocer in the village, and Saturday's the only day Mr. Crisp's at home to drive the car and can bring her in."

"What about the other Miss Hyland then—Miss Julie Hyland?" Constance asked. "Couldn't she have kept the place open?"

Mrs. Newcome gave a faint shake of her head. "She probably wouldn't care to do that. She'd help her sister a bit if she was at home, but she never did care for the work. If Miss Jennifer didn't come home when she was expected, I think Miss Julie might have closed the place."

"But only after Mr. Greer called."

"That's right."

"It's rather odd, isn't it?"

"That's what I can't help thinking."

"Do you know what time it was when you saw him go into the café?"

"Not really. Some time between two and half past, I'd say. I didn't happen to look at my watch."

"Well, I'd certainly tell the police about it," Constance said. "There's probably some quite simple explanation, but anything to do with that café on Saturday might be important."

Mrs. Newcome gave a sigh and stood up.

"I was really hoping you'd tell me I needn't bother about it," she said, "but I suppose even if you had, I'd have gone on worrying about it. So it's best for me to get it over and be done with it. I think I'll go along to the police station now."

"My daughter and I are just going out," Constance said. "We're taking the car. I could drive you there if that would help you."

"That's very kind. Thank you. Yes, it would be a help."

Mrs. Newcome appeared very grateful for the lift, but her presence in the car prevented Constance and Irene discussing the information that she had given them, and after they had left her at the police station, they drove straight to the shop called Conrad Greer, Antiques, were fortunate in finding parking-space near it, and went into the shop.

It was in an arcade, for pedestrians only. Most of the other shops in the arcade were antique shops or sold china and glassware, expensive-looking confections, or fabulously costly woollen goods. Conrad Greer's shop was one of the largest there. It had a window on either side of its door, and as Constance and Irene entered, Greer himself, with the assistance of Julie Hyland, was moving a bow-fronted chest of drawers into one of the windows. He looked up at Constance, smiled, and said, "I'll be with you in a moment." Then he continued to manoeuvre the moderately massive yet elegant-looking piece of furniture into the exact place that he wanted for it.

Julie Hyland looked round at them and said, "Good morning," then, when the chest of drawers had been deposited where Greer wanted, she began to wander round the shop, looking for ornaments to put on top of it to create an attractive display. She found a flowery soup tureen and some silver candlesticks which satisfied her and arranged them carefully while Greer came to greet Constance and Irene.

Constance introduced Irene. He held out a hand to her, but withdrew it before she had taken it, saying, "Sorry, my hands are dirty. I've just been polishing up that chest. Nice, don't you think? It's Biedermeier. To get a really good price for it, I'll have to send it to Germany. They're buying back all they can of their own antiques, which they parted with for a song when times were hard for them."

"So you send some of your things abroad, do you?" Constance said.

His gaze sharpened slightly at the question. "Oh, they've been telling you about that, have they? I've sent a good deal of stuff to Ken and Margot in Sydney. Does that seem strange to you?"

"It's nothing to do with me," she answered. She looked round the shop and found a chair on which she thought that it would be safe to sit down.

Irene wandered across the shop to examine the chest of drawers in the window.

"I mean, that the Paulings and I should have been on good enough terms to have business dealings after what happened in the past," Greer said. "You know all about that by now, I assume. That Colin was my son. And you were there when I walked in and found Margot there, and you saw that that was quite a shock to me. Not an altogether agreeable shock. It's one thing to be corresponding with people at the other end of the world and receiving the occasional cheque from them and another to find yourself, without warning, face to face. I imagine if poor Margot had lived, we'd be on friendly enough terms by now. Our affair didn't go deep, you know. She was a bit of a nympho, as Pauling no doubt later discovered to his cost. If Colin hadn't arrived, I don't suppose he'd ever have known anything about her and me. Now what else do you want to know?"

His tone was bitter. Constance made an embarrassed gesture with one hand.

"I'm sorry, that isn't what I came to ask you about at all," she said.

"You don't want to know if I'm a receiver of stolen property?"

She saw the stormy look in his eyes and tried to defend herself against it with a smile.

"Well, are you?" she asked.

For a moment he seemed to be taken aback by the question; then he laughed.

"Forgive me," he said. "You're quite right, of course. If I were, I shouldn't tell you. But you do know those chessmen I was going to give Colin were stolen, don't you?"

"So Mr. Frayne told me."

"And for all I know, that chair you're sitting on was stolen. I bought a set of six like that at an auction, but I didn't inquire into how they got there. But now tell me, why did you come in here this morning? It wasn't just as a customer, was it?"

Irene had turned back from the window and was standing beside Constance. Before Constance could reply, she said, "Actually it was. I'm getting married, and we're here to choose a wedding-present if we can find something that appeals to us. What's that over there?"

She was pointing at a plate propped up on a shelf. It had a bold floral pattern of an unusual shade of green on a creamy background and was very attractive, Constance thought, though it seemed to her too modest a thing to be an adequate wedding-present.

"It's Marseilles faience," Greer answered. "I wasn't sure what it was myself, so I had it identified by Sotheby's."

"Is it very expensive?" Irene asked.

"To a friend, I'd part with it for forty-five pounds," he said, smiling, "but you don't want it, do you? You want to know if I murdered poor little Jennifer Hyland."

"I don't," Irene said sharply, "because I know who did. But if you don't want to sell us that plate, you've only to say so."

"What the hell d'you mean, you know who did it?" he demanded. The smile had quite gone. "You're here just out of curiosity, aren't you? You're drawn by the smell of murder. It pulls at you and excites you, like a hound on the trail of a fox. And you'd like to be in at the kill, wouldn't you? You'd like to get your teeth into the poor bloody beast and pull it to pieces. People like you make me sick. If you want that plate, all right, you can have it for nothing. Get Julie to wrap it up for you and take it away. But I'm going out now. I've things to do, and I don't want to waste my time on people who don't even honestly say what they really want with me. Julie, give them the plate."

With a black scowl on his face, he strode out of the shop.

Eight

Irene looked at Julie with an expression of bewilderment on her face.

"Now what made him explode like that?" she said. "How did I upset him?"

Julie gave a curious smile.

"Do you want the plate?" she asked.

"Not like that," Irene said. "I mean, we'll buy it for forty-five pounds, if that's what it's worth, but I don't want it for nothing. Not like that."

"You don't seem to know when you're in luck," Julie said. She looked at Constance. "You don't really want anything, do you?"

"Not really, no," Constance replied.

"I'm sorry, he's in a very nervous state," Julie said. "You can hardly blame him, can you?"

It seemed to Constance that in view of the fact that Julie's sister had been murdered only two days ago, she herself was surprisingly calm. She stood leaning against the Biedermeier chest with her hands in the pockets of the well-fitting slacks that she was wearing, and she met Constance's eyes with a sardonic glint in her own. Her handsome face was perhaps a little paler than when Constance had seen her last, and there was a hollowness about her cheeks that had not been there then; but she seemed tired rather than tense and did not look in the least likely to explode like her employer, partner, or whatever he was.

"Has he been much bothered by the police?" Constance asked.

"A certain amount," Julie answered, "but not actually about the murders. They asked him where he was at the time Colin started shooting and he hasn't any alibi, and they know that he and Margot had an affair years ago and that Colin was their son, but they didn't really seem much interested in all that. It's the question of whether or not he knew that some chessmen he was going to give Colin were stolen that they've really been battering him about. And if he did know, then did he know perhaps that other things we've been handling were stolen? In other words, has he been a receiver of stolen property for Heaven knows how long? Having that happen on top of the murders has been just a bit too much for him. He really loved that boy, you know."

"Haven't the police been at you too about receiving the stolen property?" Irene asked.

It was the kind of question that Constance could not have brought herself to ask, but Irene had all too few inhibitions when her curiosity happened to have been aroused.

Julie's gaze moved from Constance's face to Irene's with deepening irony in it.

"Indeed yes," she answered. "I'm a very suspicious character."

"Have you ever suspected that Greer was a fence?" Irene asked.

"Since you ask me, yes, I have sometimes wondered," Julie replied without giving any sign of taking offence at the question. "He bought a good deal of stuff from some rather shady characters. But he isn't a suspicious man himself, and if they offered him things cheap, he'd more probably think they didn't know the value of what they were handling and that it was a bargain for him. And his wanting to give those chessmen to the boy suggests he didn't know they were stolen."

"Except that criminals nearly always think they can get away with everything, don't they?" Irene said. "I mean, they'd never take the risks they do if they thought seriously there was much chance of their being caught."

"Criminal!" Julie gave an abrupt little laugh. "It's so extraordinary to think of applying the word to Conrad."

"But don't you think it's possible he might have assumed it was quite safe to give the chessmen to Colin because no one who could know anything about where they came from was ever going to see them?"

Before Julie could answer, Constance said quickly, "But he knew the police were in the house when he brought them in the afternoon."

Julie was looking thoughtful. She took some time to respond. Then she said, "I don't really know the answer to that. Did he bring them because he was quite innocent and didn't know they were stolen or because he took for granted he could get away with it, as your daughter's suggested, even with the police in the house? I've sometimes wondered about . . ." But then she paused and withdrew her gaze from Irene, looking frowningly before her at nothing in particular.

"Yes?" Constance prompted her after a moment.

"Tell me, what did you think of the Barrows?" Julie asked.

It was not a question that Constance had been expecting.

"I thought they were very charming people," she said. "Kind and generous."

"Both of them?"

"Why, yes."

"Of course, you only knew Mrs. Barrow when she was ill."

"What has that got to do with it?"

"Don't you think people sometimes get quite unlike themselves when they're ill?" Julie said.

Constance was puzzled.

"Yes, I suppose some of them get very crotchety and irritable," she answered. "But certainly that didn't happen to Mrs. Barrow. She was very undemanding and always very grateful for even little things that were done for her."

"That's what I mean," Julie said. "When she was well, she was quite a Tartar. But people like that may get frightened when they're ill. They know they're in your power, and they aren't used to it and don't really trust you to be kind to them. So they set about propitiating you in every way they can think of, and people who are really very domineering and perhaps downright dangerous in their way become ever so sweet and gentle. Haven't you seen that happen?"

"I may have," Constance said, "but I don't understand what you're talking about. Are you implying that poor little Mrs. Barrow could be dangerous to anyone?"

Julie withdrew a hand from her pocket and with one

finger began tracing the marquetry pattern on the top of the Biedermeier chest. She looked down, still frowning, at what she was doing, as if it needed care.

"I'll tell you an odd thing that used to happen," she said. "Perhaps I ought not to say anything about it, but I know you've got involved in the whole thing just by being on the spot, so I don't see why I shouldn't talk to you. From time to time, you see, Mrs. Barrow used to come into the shop with Colin. When that happened, Conrad would nearly always send me out of the shop with Colin, and I'd take him along to the confectioner in the arcade and buy him sweets or something. And it was a bit difficult, because he didn't like me and he'd be horribly sullen the whole time. Then, when we got back here, Mrs. Barrow would be just ready to leave and would be smiling and cheerful and so grateful for the sweets I'd bought for Colin and would tell him to thank me nicely and so on. But the moment she and Colin had gone, Conrad would show that he was in a foul temper and would snap my head off and probably rush out of the shop, just as he did this morning, and go to the pub round the corner and start sinking whiskys till he was hardly fit to work for the rest of the day. And once I heard him mutter, 'I'm going to kill that woman!'" She broke off and gave a deep sigh. "There, I know I oughtn't to have started telling you about this. You'll think I'm trying to suggest it was the murder of Mrs. Barrow that Jennifer saw, not Margot's, and that Conrad's guilty. But I never meant to say anything of the sort."

"What I think you're suggesting," Constance said, "is that Mrs. Barrow may have been blackmailing him because she'd somehow found out about his receiving stolen things, and when she came here on the visits that upset him so badly, she was making him pay her for her silence. Isn't that it?''

Julie tucked her hand back into her pocket. Her whole posture had changed. It had become rigidly challenging, as if she were prepared to defend herself against some onslaught. Her frown looked angry rather than abstracted.

"Of course, I don't believe a word of it," Constance said. "What interests me is why you told me such a story."

Julie did not reply.

"What did she buy when she came here?" Irene asked.

"Nothing," Julie answered.

"Nothing ever?"

"No."

"I mean, she wasn't collecting some special kind of thing and just didn't buy anything if Conrad didn't happen to have what she wanted in stock?"

"I told you, no."

"Then perhaps Mr. Greer got into a foul temper with her because he felt she was wasting his time," Constance suggested. "He's got a fairly volatile temper, hasn't he?"

Julie caught her breath again, managing to get rid of her frown and then even to smile a little.

"You know, that's what I used to think myself," she said. "It's just the atmosphere at the moment that makes one . . . Well, I've had such horrible thoughts going through my head ever since they found poor Jennifer's body. Its being found so near Conrad's house— No, there I go again, suggesting things. Please take no notice of what I've been saying. I'm simply not myself at the moment."

"You aren't the only person who's pointed out that it

wasn't far from the pool where they found your sister's body to Conrad's house," Irene said. "And there's the point that if he had nothing to do with her death, someone else had to get away from the pool and back to the village without being seen, unless it was a hitch-hiker who went in the opposite direction."

"Who said anything about that?" Julie asked sharply.

"Kenneth Pauling."

Julie raised her eyebrows, but said nothing. Constance stood up.

"We're wasting your time," she said. "If you'd like that plate, Irene—"

"No, no, no," Irene broke in. "I don't want it. I don't want anything."

"Because you've got what you came for?" Julie asked.

She and Irene stared at one another; then Irene shook her head.

"More than we came for, really, but I'm not sure if it's any use." She took Constance by the arm and guided her out of the shop.

They were in the car, on the way back to Constance's house, before either of them spoke again. Irene had a dreamy air, as if her thoughts had drifted far away, before Constance at last asked, "What did you mean by saying we'd got more than we came for? It didn't seem to me we'd got much. But then I'm not sure why we went there at all."

"Tell me something," Irene said. "You knew Mrs. Barrow. I know she was a sick woman and perhaps wasn't quite her normal self, but can you imagine her being a blackmailer?"

"Didn't I tell Julie I didn't believe her?"

"That's what I thought. She was really a nice old lady, was she?"

"Very nice."

"So the whole of what that Hyland woman told us about her was a lie. That's what I meant by saying we'd got more than we came for. We know now she's a liar."

"But it may not all have been lies, you know," Constance said.

"What do you mean?"

"Well, suppose it was quite true that Mrs. Barrow used to come into the shop from time to time, bringing Colin with her and knowing, of course, that Conrad Greer was Colin's father. Mightn't she have had some reason for coming to see him which had nothing to do with blackmail?"

"Such as?"

"Perhaps she just wanted to consult him about Colin's upbringing, or perhaps Greer contributed to Colin's keep and used to pay her then, without its having anything to do with blackmail. I don't think the Barrows were specially well off."

"Why wouldn't Greer pay them in their own home? He came there fairly often, didn't he?"

"Perhaps the colonel didn't know of the arrangement. And if Greer could help them with Colin, it may have been welcome."

"Or perhaps she never came at all."

They had come to a halt in front of Constance's house. Constance looked into Irene's face, which had been turned away from her with an expression of deep thoughtfulness.

"Is that what you really think?" Constance asked.

"I'd be inclined to think so if I could think of a motive for her having told us that yarn," Irene said.

"It would mean she's got some reason for wanting to get Greer into trouble, wouldn't it?" Constance said.

"Oh yes, that's what she was trying to do, that's obvious."

"It's odd, because I'd been given the impression by the colonel that she and Greer have probably had an affair going on over the years. It wouldn't be surprising if they had, because they've worked together for a long time and she's an attractive woman."

"Perhaps the trouble is that they haven't had an affair going on and she wants to take her revenge for that. On the other hand, suppose she's been blackmailing him herself and now wants to cover her tracks by getting people to believe Mrs. Barrow was the trouble-maker."

"You believe Greer's a fence, do you, and has always known he was handling stolen property?"

"Oh yes, that's evident. What I'm not sure of is . . ." Irene stopped, opened the car door beside her, and stepped out into the street.

Constance got out of the car too and locked it.

"What aren't you sure of?" she asked as they walked up the path to her front door.

"It's just that I've been wondering if I made a mistake yesterday," Irene said. "I was completely sure that Pauling was the murderer of his wife and Jennifer. I could feel it in my bones. But now— Well, I'm not ready to say I was wrong, but I'm equally sure now that Greer's capable of murder. I don't say he committed these two particular murders in Long Meldon, but I'm sure he could have."

"If luckily for him someone else hadn't done it first, you mean."

"Now you're laughing at me," Irene said. "You always laugh at me. Why don't you ever take me seriously?"

"But often I do. It's just that sometimes I find it rather difficult."

Constance had taken her latchkey out of her handbag and unlocked the door before them. It was true that she found it difficult to take seriously the feelings in Irene's bones, and at the moment she would have been grateful if that morning the two of them had somehow stumbled on some solid evidence about the murders. But solid evidence was a job for the police, not for her and Irene, and the murders were not her business at all. She had told the police all that she knew about them, and if there was anything more that they wanted from her, they knew where to find her.

Stepping into the house, followed by Irene, she closed the door behind them and went to the kitchen to consider that ever recurring problem, what were they going to eat for lunch? She thought that she would make omelettes and that before starting on them they might have some sherry.

It worried her, however, as she took sherry and glasses into the sitting-room, where she found Irene slumped in a chair, staring broodingly before her, that some thought that in the morning had been clear to her had since eluded her. She knew that it had interested her briefly and that she had intended to think more about it later, but other things had distracted her and now she could not remember what it had been. Probably it had not been anything important. If it had been, it would no doubt suddenly return to her while she was thinking about something else.

Holding her glass of sherry, she sat down, observing, "I'm getting old."

Irene did not appear to think it necessary to reply to this undeniable statement.

"My memory," Constance went on, "is not what it used to be."

"I should say it's reasonably good, considering," Irene said with some indifference, still plainly pursuing some line of thought of her own. "I don't often catch you out."

"But I catch myself out," Constance said. "Where there ought to be some quite clear idea in my mind, there's sometimes just a blank. For instance, this morning . . ." But suddenly as she said that the lost thought came back to her. "It's all right, I know what I wanted to say. It was about something Mrs. Newcome said to me. Do you remember her telling us about seeing Greer in the village in the afternoon?"

"Yes." Irene sipped her sherry. "And I suppose she's told the police about it by now. Does it matter?"

"It's only that there's something a little odd about it," Constance said. "He came to Riverside in the afternoon, bringing the chessmen for Colin, and he came on foot. But when Mrs. Newcome saw him, he was in his car. So why didn't he come to Riverside by car on his way home? I know what you'll say. You'll say he'd forgotten to bring the chessmen with him and had to go home for them. But if he'd done that and had driven up the lane to his house, he'd have seen that Riverside was already crawling with policemen. And wouldn't it have been the normal thing for him to do then to stop and find out what was going on? But he didn't. He drove home, then quite a bit later arrived on foot, carrying the chessmen and making out that the sight of the police quite surprised him."

"Doesn't that mean he didn't know the chessmen were stolen?"

"That's how it looks."

"Actually I was just thinking about that trip of his to the village," Irene said, "but what I was wondering about is why he went there. Mrs. Newcome told us he stopped at the café, went in and came out again almost immediately, I suppose because he found nobody there

—so where was Julie when he did that? We know where Jennifer was. She was dead in the pool. And Mrs. Crisp was in Bracklington with her husband, shopping. But where was Julie?"

"I telephoned the café early in the afternoon wanting to speak to Jennifer, and Julie answered, so she was there then," Constance said.

"You're sure of that?" Irene asked. "I mean, that it was Julie?" Irene asked.

"Oh yes."

"So it looks as if it wasn't Julie that he wanted to see. But if it was Jennifer, then he can't have been the person who pushed her into the pool. The fact that the pool's so near his house and that it would have been easier for him than for anyone else to get away from where she was left really doesn't mean anything. I believe my first feeling was right after all. It was Ken Pauling who did it. And he simply walked away and came back to the village, and it just happened that nobody saw him. Unless, of course, somebody did see him and is keeping quiet about it."

"Who are you thinking of?"

"Nobody in particular. It was just a thought."

Irene did not explain herself further, for just then the door bell rang.

It was Detective Inspector Frayne who stood on the doorstep.

Constance invited him into the house, took him to the sitting-room, and introduced him to Irene. She greeted him with a look of deep distrust. In the world in which she had been living for some years, the police were normally regarded as the enemy. He did not seem to notice it and said that he was glad that her mother had her company at this very difficult time. But he did not seem much interested in her.

Taking the chair that Constance offered him while she herself sat down again, he said, "You remember, Mrs. Lawley, I asked you some questions about the set of fire irons in the Barrows' drawing-room?"

She nodded.

"And I told you," he went on, "that a shovel and tongs were there, but no poker."

"Yes."

"Well, we've found the poker. It was among some shrubs outside the back door of the house."

"And you believe it was what was used to knock Jennifer Hyland unconscious."

"We're sure of it. There are blood stains and a few hairs on it. The hairs match hers, and the blood is the same group as hers."

"May I ask you then why you've taken the trouble to come and tell me about it?" Constance said. "I don't mean I'm not interested, but I should have thought that from your point of view it would be a waste of time."

"There's a question I want to ask you," he said. "Something I want to check up on. I believe on Saturday morning you went into the village to do some shopping, met Mr. Pauling, and had coffee with him in Jenny's Café."

"That's correct," she said.

"But Miss Jennifer Hyland had already left the café before you went into it."

"Yes, I saw her driving away."

"Then who waited on you?"

"Jennifer's sister, Julie."

"And when you left, you went into the shop across the way and were there for some time."

"I think I told you that, didn't I?"

"Yes, you did. But you were puzzled about why it seemed to have taken Jennifer Hyland so long to reach the Barrows' house. There was something like half an hour unaccounted for. Well, we have the answer to that now."

"So have I. She spent it with Mrs. Newcome, didn't she? She was here this morning and told us about it. She also told us about having seen Mr. Greer in the village, going into the café and coming out of it again. She didn't seem to know if it could be of any importance, nor did I, but I advised her to tell you about it. In fact, I gave her a lift to the police station."

"So she told me and that's partly why I'm here. Assuming that Miss Hyland didn't arrive at Riverside until a short time before you got back there, because of her having spent some time with Mrs. Newcome, there was time before she arrived for someone to get from the village to the house and witness the murders by the boy Colin and add another of his own to them, even if he'd been in the café with you until the time when you went into the grocer's."

"You're talking of Mr. Pauling."

"Of course he is," Irene said with a touch of weariness in her tone, as if she thought this a matter about which too much had been said already. "I know you can't arrest him till you've something solid to go on, but you know he's guilty, don't you? There's just one thing that puzzles me."

He appeared for the first time to take an interest in her.

"Yes?" he said.

"Why didn't he shoot Jennifer if he wanted to get rid of her? Why did he take to using a poker?"

"For a very simple reason, Miss Lawley," he said. "The gun was empty."

"I don't understand," she said. "Colin shot his grandparents and himself and then Pauling shot Margot—that's four bullets. Doesn't a gun hold more bullets than that?"

"In this case, six," he answered. "But we've found two bullets embedded in the wall of the drawing-room to one side of the fireplace, near to where the colonel's body was. Colin, it would appear, was not a very good shot. He wasted two bullets. So when the other character, whoever it was, came in, found himself face to face with Margot Pauling, and shot her, he was using the last bullet in the gun."

"So when he discovered there was a witness to this, he had to use something else to get rid of her, and as it happens, it was the poker." Irene sounded excited. "And he couldn't leave her just lying there, could he? That would have shown you at once that there'd been another murderer in the room besides Colin."

"Exactly."

"Dragging her body out to the car and then pushing it into the pool must have taken some strength," she said. "Pauling's a fairly powerful man, I should say."

"You've met him then?" he asked.

"Oh yes."

"And you're convinced he murdered his wife and Jennifer Hyland?"

For once Irene looked a little embarrassed.

"It's just an idea of mine," she said. "If I explained why I think it, you wouldn't understand me."

"Why not try me?" he suggested.

She shook her head. "It's nothing that would interest you. I mean, unless you've had some experience yourself of finding out you just know something, you can't explain it."

"But I've often had that experience," he said, "only it

generally turns out I've been wrong. Naturally it's just the times when I've been right that I like to remember. But perhaps your intuitions are more efficient than mine."

He must be basically a kind man, Constance thought, even if his profession had hardened him.

He turned back to her. "So you and Mr. Pauling were waited on in the café by Julie Hyland, so you can give her an alibi."

"Julie Hyland—an alibi!" Constance exclaimed. "Have you really been thinking she could have been the murderer?"

"We've been thinking of everybody," he said, "even the butcher and the baker and the candlestick maker. The grocer, you may be interested to hear, can confirm that you came into his shop at about eleven o'clock and spent a longish time there."

"So you've even been checking up on me!"

"Oh yes."

"But I believe that if I had hit someone on the head with a poker, I'd hardly have made a dent. I'm reasonably strong, but not up to knocking a person out. And I could never have dragged the poor girl's body to the car."

"And you hadn't time to do it, which is perhaps the most convincing reason why you can't be under suspicion." He stood up. "It's an annoying thing, in view of the fact that he may well be guilty, that Mr. Pauling has disappeared. He walked out of the Green Dragon yesterday evening and hasn't been seen since. He may be a person who got on to a bus into Bracklington, but the identification isn't positive. However, we'll catch up with him without much difficulty, I imagine, but it's a waste of valuable time and very irritating. Well, thank you, Mrs. Lawley, and you, Miss Lawley."

He did not wait as Constance got hurriedly to her feet to go to the front door and let him out, but turned quickly, left the sitting-room, and let himself out of the house.

Constance sank down in her chair and reached for her sherry.

"So it looks as if you may have been right after all," she said.

"That Pauling must be guilty because he's disappeared?" Irene said.

"Well, why else should he go?"

"I can think of all sorts of reasons, though they don't affect my view of him. One, he might just have wanted to get home to Australia. Two, that he knew of some evidence against someone else, probably Conrad Greer, realised he's in danger because of it, and got out while he could. Three, he didn't much like the Green Dragon and he's gone to look for some better hotel. Four, he's been murdered and his body hasn't been found yet. Five, he's found he can't live with his conscience and has committed suicide. Six—"

"Stop!" Constance cried. "You still think he's guilty."

"I'm not as sure of that as I was since meeting Conrad Greer. If I hadn't already met Pauling, I'd be sure Greer was the murderer."

"Or Mrs. Barrow, as Julie suggested."

"Of course not. That was all moonshine. If anyone was blackmailing Greer, I'd guess it was Julie herself, or perhaps she was just going shares with him in the proceeds of his receiving and wanted to put all the blame she could on him, just to clear herself, as the thing seemed to be coming out. But you didn't tell that man Frayne anything about what Julie said. Was that because you didn't believe it?"

"I think it was really because I was thinking of something else," Constance said. "It's something that's been puzzling me, though I haven't really thought about it. Look, what the police believe is that Jennifer went out to Riverside to deliver Colin's cake and that she arrived just in time to see someone take the gun that Colin had dropped and shoot someone with it, probably Margot. But what would you have done yourself if you'd seen a thing like that? Would you have stayed around to be hit on the head with a poker?"

"I'd have bolted for my life," Irene said.

Constance nodded. "So should I—unless I was feeling very brave and dashed into the dining-room, where there's a telephone, and dialled 999. But I think I'd have bolted, jumped into my car, and driven off to the police as fast as I could."

Irene looked at her uncertainly. "But she didn't do that, so what do you think really happened?"

"The only thing I can think of is that the murderer, as soon as he realised she was there, threatened her with the gun, which she didn't realise was empty, then snatched up the poker and hit her with it."

"But didn't hit her hard enough to kill her with it. He only knocked her unconscious, then carried her out to her car, and drove off to the pool. Of course he had to remove her from the scene, but why didn't he kill her outright, then carry her out?"

"Because he was in a hurry. He knew I'd be getting back to the house soon and wanted to get away before I arrived."

"And who would have known that?"

"I suppose Pauling."

Irene gave a hollow little laugh. "So you're coming round to my view after all. You've taken your time about it, looking for so-called solid evidence instead of just trusting to your instincts, which is really so much wiser. But at least you agree with me now. You really do, don't you, Mum?"

"The only trouble is, I don't think anyone could call that really solid evidence," Constance replied. "There may have been several other people who'd heard I was working for the Barrows and saw me in the village and knew for sure I'd be getting back soon. Conrad Greer may have seen me. Julie did. Mrs. Crisp did. Mrs. Newcome perhaps."

"It's got to be someone strong," Irene said. "Strong enough to carry Jennifer's body to the car. And you've said yourself Julie has an alibi. So was it Pauling or Greer?"

Constance stood up. "I think I'll go and get the lunch," she said. "We'll never get anywhere talking like this."

She went out to the kitchen to make the omelettes.

She was glad that when lunch was over Irene found a book on one of Constance's bookshelves that she appeared inclined to read. She settled down on the sofa with her feet up and showed no desire to go on talking. Curious as to what might interest Irene at such a time, Constance glanced over her shoulder to see what the book was and saw that it was an old copy that she had forgotten that she possessed of Stevenson's *Travels with a Donkey in the Cévennes.* Constance remembered that Irene had spoken of going travelling with Samuel on bicycles or on foot and wondered if it had occurred to her that a donkey might be a more interesting form of transport than either.

It did not seem unlike her. She seemed deeply absorbed in the book, for which Constance was grateful. She felt too restless to be able to read herself, but she had some knitting which had been lying about in the

room for some time and to which she occasionally
added a few rows, and she thought that doing this now
might be calming. But she had no sooner picked it up
and sat down with it than the telephone rang.

"Mrs. Lawley?" It was the voice of Mrs. Jay from the
Bracklington Helpers. "I've been reading the terrible
news about the house I sent you to last week. My dear,
I can't tell you how sorry I feel to have got you involved
in such a dreadful thing. I know in our work we can
sometimes run into very strange situations, but you
aren't really involved in all this, are you?"

"If you mean, am I suspected of the murders or have
I been helping the police with their inquiries, well no, I
don't think I've helped them much and I don't think
I'm suspected of anything," Constance replied. "But I
was thinking of ringing you up to ask if I'm going to be
paid for the full week I was engaged for or only for the
time I actually spent at Riverside, because of course I
haven't done the full time. We can forget the whole
thing, if you like, because I certainly haven't done a
normal amount of work."

"Of course you'll be paid for the full time," Mrs. Jay
said. "I'm sure what you've been through has been
much more wearing than the hardest kind of work. But
you're all right, are you? I mean, the shock hasn't been
too great for you. Do you think you'd be up to doing
another job?"

"No, oh no, I couldn't possibly," Constance said
swiftly. "I'm sorry, but I just feel I've got to stay at
home very quietly."

"I understand, of course. I was just hoping . . .
Such a nice young couple, you know, and they really
need help."

"The Barrows were a very nice old couple, but all the
help I could give them didn't do much."

"This is different. The poor girl had a fall and broke three ribs. She did it falling out of bed, would you believe it? Such an odd accident. And they've a dear little boy—"

"I'm not going anywhere again where there are children, Mrs. Jay," Constance interrupted.

"Oh, that doesn't sound like you, Mrs. Lawley," Mrs. Jay said. "Of course, I know you must need a rest and I won't press you, but if you should change your mind . . . The fact is, we seem to have had an epidemic of accidents and operations and illnesses of all kinds, and we don't seem to have any spare helpers at the moment, and I do so hate refusing people. Well, perhaps I can find someone else. Take care of yourself, won't you? Do you know if the police have any idea who killed the girl they found in the pond?"

"If they have, they haven't confided in me," Constance said.

"But they believe it was because she witnessed those murders in the house, don't they? That's what it said in the paper. You didn't actually witness anything yourself, did you?"

"Nothing at all. I just walked into a room and found four dead bodies there."

"Terrible, terrible! Well, as I said, take care of yourself. I'm so glad you didn't actually witness anything. And I suppose nobody can think you did."

Constance said firmly, "Nobody," and Mrs. Jay said goodbye and rang off.

Constance returned to her knitting. But as she picked it up, she scowled at it, partly because she felt confused about the pattern, but also because Mrs. Jay's concern for her safety had suddenly made her wonder if in fact it was possible that whoever had struck so devastatingly at Riverside could believe for a moment that she had seen or knew something more than she actually did.

And did she in fact know something more than she realised?

Her mouth took on a hard line as she tried to concentrate on the complicated pattern that she had chosen for her knitting, mistakenly, for she was not really an expert knitter, while at the same time attempting to discover why she should have the uncomfortable feeling that she knew something that was eluding her grasp. She had one of her attacks once more of feeling that her memory was not what it had been. But was there really anything to remember? She might be simply the victim of strain and weariness which left her feeling guiltily inadequate to cope with the situation in which she was trapped.

She knitted on doggedly for some time. Then suddenly she said, "Irene, I told that inspector a lie."

Irene grunted. Her book was lying flat on her stomach, and she was sound asleep.

Constance raised her voice, "Irene!"

"What? Oh yes—did you say something?" Irene blinked at her.

"I said I told Frayne a lie."

"That's funny," Irene said. "You don't often tell lies. You're a very truthful person."

"I didn't mean to do it. It was sheer stupidity on my part."

"Well, what was it?"

"I said that Julie Hyland waited on Pauling and me when we had coffee in Jenny's Café, and that gave her an alibi."

"Yes."

"But she didn't. She took our order, but it was Mrs. Crisp who brought the coffee and later on our bill. Perhaps Mrs. Crisp can give Julie an alibi. She may know that she was out in the kitchen all the morning, but all I can say myself is that she took our order and then disappeared."

"Are you saying that Julie murdered Margot and then her sister?"

"I'm only saying that perhaps she could have done it."

"But she couldn't have known there'd be a gun lying around handy, could she? That's one of the things that's been worrying me about Pauling. How did he know there'd be a gun there? It looks as if Julie, if she did go up to the house while you were having coffee and then doing your shopping, can't have had any intention of committing murder."

"I know. All the same, I think I'm going along to the police station and tell them I've misled them."

"What, now?"

"Yes," Constance said, putting down her knitting and standing up.

"Oh dear," Irene said, "I'm so sleepy."

"You needn't come."

"Oh, I'll come. I feel happier keeping an eye on you."

"Of course, I'm remembering that it would have taken someone with a good deal of strength to get Jennifer into her car and then push her into the pool."

"Are you thinking about the Biedermeier?"

"The what?" Constance asked.

"The Biedermeier chest in Conrad Greer's shop. Didn't you notice it?"

"You don't mean you think it was stolen? I should think it was too big. Most of the things taken from that house in Granwich were probably quite small, which the burglar could carry away with him."

Irene swung her legs to the ground. "One does hear

of furniture vans arriving outside houses where the
owners have gone away and clearing the places out. The
neighbours don't take any notice, because they think
the owners are simply moving away. But if that chest
was stolen, I don't suppose it would have been put into
the shop window. It would more probably be on its way
to Australia by now."

"Why did you mention it then?"

"Oh, just a thought."

"Well, if we're going to the police station, the sooner
we get going, the better."

Constance felt that even if what she had to tell
Frayne was a matter of no interest to him—if, for instance, Mrs. Crisp had been able to say that Julie had
been in the kitchen of the café all the morning—she
would still feel easier in her mind when she had cor-
rected what she had told him before.

She picked up her handbag, took her car keys out of
it, went to the front door, and opened it.

Kenneth Pauling had just got out of a taxi at the gate
and came walking up the path towards her.

Nine

Constance paused in the doorway, then made a gesture, inviting him to come in. She said nothing. Irene did not say anything either. She looked at him with an intent, penetrating gaze while he hardly looked at her. Making a fist of one of his hands, he raised it and stared at it as if there were something that he felt he ought to be able to do with it, though he was not sure what.

After a moment Constance said, "Where have you been? The police have been looking for you."

"I've only been to London," he said. "I wanted to see an old friend of mine, someone I knew before I went to Australia. A solicitor. I saw him this morning. I wanted his help in case I get arrested for this thing. It seems I may be going to inherit the Barrows' money, which gives me a kind of motive. Also I wanted him to take over my affairs. I want to get back to Australia as soon as they'll let me go, but if there's anything for me to inherit, I don't want to throw it away."

"Do you think you're going to be arrested?" Constance asked.

He shrugged his shoulders. "I think anything could happen, but I'm not running away from it."

"That's what the police thought you were doing," she said.

"I've come back again, haven't I?"

Irene was still eyeing him with doubt and suspicion in her glance.

"But why just here?" she asked. "What do you want with my mother?"

"Ah, that's what I'd better explain," he said. "You remember our having coffee on Saturday morning, Mrs. Lawley?"

"Yes, of course," she said.

"Do you remember that Julie Hyland took our order that morning, but afterwards we were waited on by a little woman in a pink overall?"

"Mrs. Crisp," she said. "Yes."

"Well, I had a talk with Mrs. Crisp yesterday evening before I left for London, and I asked her if Julie Hyland had in fact been in the café all the morning or if she'd left it. Mrs. Crisp said she hadn't seen her and had had to manage on her own."

"It's a funny thing, but Irene and I were just on our way to the police to tell them about that," Constance said. "I mean, that the alibi I'd given Julie didn't hold water. But I haven't spoken to Mrs. Crisp, so I didn't know if perhaps Julie had spent the rest of the morning in the kitchen."

"She didn't," he said. "And I came here to ask you to come to the police with me to support me when I tell them about Julie disappearing from the café after she'd taken our orders."

"Yes, of course, I'll do that," Constance said. "But why do you think she did that? Where did she go?"

"My belief is she went up to Greer's house to have a talk with him about Margot and got him to go to Riverside to tell her that the old affair wasn't going to start again. I think Julie was very frightened that it might. She'd had an affair with him herself for years, but she may have known that the one he'd had with Margot all that time ago had meant far more to him than she ever had, particularly in view of their having had the child, whom that man really loved. And Julie told him that you were in the village, so you wouldn't be around to overhear them talking, and she guessed the old people wouldn't eavesdrop, because they were probably still hoping, for the child's sake, that his affair with Margot could be patched up, and she said that if he didn't do what she wanted she was going to tip the police off that he'd been receiving stolen property for years. He was pretty much in her power. So he went along and walked into the house just as Colin started his campaign of murder. And what happened then . . ." He had dropped his fist, and his gaze was fastened with a strange, sightless brilliance on Constance's face. "I don't know what happened," he added lamely. "It's possible he and Margot were on the terrace talking. I believe they've deduced she was out there by the cigarette stubs in the ashtray on the table. And the two of them may have gone running into the room when the shooting started, and Greer tried to get the gun away from Colin and somehow shot Margot by accident. I don't want to blame a man who's innocent in his way . . ." He paused, then added explosively, "But I

don't believe it! I believe he shot Margot in cold
blood!"

"And Jennifer walked in on the scene and so had to
be silenced and disposed of."

"Yes." He rubbed a hand across his eyes. He looked
exceedingly tired, as if he had not slept much during
his night in London. "God, why didn't I go up to the
house myself that morning? I nearly did after we'd separated, you know. I thought of going there and trying to
persuade Margot to come home with me. Perhaps I'd
have been too late even if I'd done that, but I might
have saved the girl. However, it's not much good thinking about that now. Will you come to the police with
me?"

"Yes, but really this is all very hypothetical, isn't it?"
Constance said. "If you're right that Julie was in Greer's
house at the time of the murders, how did she get home
again without being seen? She was in the café when I
telephoned in the afternoon."

"But that's easy," Irene said. She had not taken her
eyes off Pauling's face from the time when he had come
into the room. She looked as if she were trying to find
out what was going on in his brain simply by using her
gaze to bore into his skull. "She came in Greer's car. Do
you remember how Mrs. Newcome told us about seeing
him drive up to the café just before she went into the
grocer's opposite? Of course, Julie was hidden in the car.
And he went quickly into the café to make certain Mrs.
Crisp wasn't there; then, at a moment when the street
was empty, Julie scrambled out of the car and shot into
the café. And Greer turned round the notice on the
door to say it was closed and drove away."

"You might think she could have walked home in an
ordinary way without all that complication after she'd
sent Greer off to talk to Margot," Constance said, "ex-

cept that I suppose she wanted to hear what he'd got to say when he got back, and when she did hear what had actually happened, she was frightened of becoming involved herself and made him take her home in the way you say."

"Are we going to the police?" Pauling said.

"Come along." Constance led the way out, and they packed themselves into the Mini.

However, when they arrived at the police station and asked for Inspector Frayne, the duty sergeant informed them that both he and Sergeant Randall were out on a case and that he knew nothing about when they might be likely to return. For a few minutes they argued about what they should do. None of them wanted to discuss the situation with a stranger who perhaps might be well informed about the Riverside case but, on the other hand, might need to have most of it explained to him. They did not know how fully the members of a local police force kept each other informed. It was surely sense, Constance said, to leave a message for Mr. Frayne, asking him to get in touch with her as soon as he returned to the police station, or even before, as she was sure the sergeant here would be able to communicate with him immediately by one of those clever radio devices so many people have now. Then the three of them could go back to her house and have some tea and wait for the inspector to arrive. Irene for once appeared to have no opinion. She had given up her deep study of Pauling's expression and, when Constance asked her what she thought they should do, only muttered in reply, "The Biedermeier . . . Yes, of course." Then she looked as if she wished that she had not said that. But Pauling was quite sure of what they should do.

"I'm going to Greer's house," he said. "If you don't

want to take me, I'll get a taxi." He turned to the sergeant. "Can I get a taxi here?"

"Sometimes," the sergeant answered not very encour-
agingly.

"It isn't far to walk," Constance said.

"All right, I'll walk."

"But, of course, we'll drive you up there," Irene said.
"I suppose you want to get your hands on Greer. I'm
sure I should if I were you. Believing what you do, I
mean."

"Don't you believe me?" he asked.

Instead of answering, she chewed the tip of a finger.

"Let's go then," Constance said and led the way back
to her car.

They did not talk as they drove to Conrad Greer's
house. Constance could sense the extreme tension in
Pauling, who was sitting beside her. When they passed
Riverside, she saw a group of people gathered at the
gate. Sightseers, she supposed, and was glad that there
was a constable there to stop them going in. She drove
on to the house beyond, and there saw that there was a
police car in the road in front of it. The three of them
got out of the Mini and, with Pauling leading them,
went up to the door on which he pounded with a heavy
iron knocker.

There was no answer. After a moment Pauling
knocked again, and there was still no answer. When he
had waited impatiently a little longer, he grasped the
door handle and turned it. The door swung open. The
sound of voices came to them from one of the rooms
inside, but these ceased as Pauling, Constance, and
Irene entered the house. Pauling strode in the direction
of the room from which the voices had come, and Constance and Irene followed him.

The room was the one in which Conrad Greer had

shown Colonel Barrow the chessmen. Greer was there, and so were Inspector Frayne and Sergeant Randall and a uniformed constable.

Seeing the intruders, Randall observed, "Christ!" It seemed that their appearance just then was a little more than he could tolerate.

Greer said, "Oh, it's you." It seemed to be a matter of indifference to him.

"Are you under arrest?" Pauling demanded aggressively.

"Mr. Greer's helping us with our inquiries," Frayne said with irony in his tone.

"Oh yes, I'm under arrest," Greer said. "They were just speaking the words of that terrible warning when you knocked." He turned to Frayne. "Would you care to repeat it? You were in the middle of it when they came."

Though his voice had a languid flatness, there was a look of desperation on his face. His eyes seemed to have sunk deep into his head. His mouth was a tight, hard line.

Wearily, as if the subject had begun to bore him, Frayne said, "Conrad Greer, I am a police officer and I arrest you for the receiving of property knowing it to be stolen, and I have to tell you that anything you say may be taken down and used as evidence at your trial."

"Receiving stolen property!" Pauling shouted. "Is that all? What about the murder of my wife?"

"I didn't murder her," Greer remarked in the same lackadaisical tone. "Yes, I've been handling stolen property and shipping it to you in Australia. And Margot knew it, if you didn't. I'm pleading guilty to that as they've already arrested the bastard who's been bringing the stuff to me for the last two or three years and he's spilled his guts about it. But I haven't murdered any-one. However, it wouldn't surprise me if you had."

Pauling's face turned a dark red. "If I could get hold of you—"

"Please, Mr. Pauling," Frayne interrupted. "Let's take this quietly. We have no evidence at the moment that Mr. Greer murdered Jennifer Hyland or your wife. Per-haps you can help us obtain some. Did you suppose your wife knew of Conrad Greer's exporting stolen property to Australia and that he had any reason to fear, when she arrived here, that she meant to expose him or possibly to blackmail him?"

"Certainly not," Pauling said. "I don't believe she knew anything about it."

"Did you?"

"Did I know about this racket of his? I did not. I assumed she was dealing with him because they were old friends."

"Friends?" Frayne said as if he found the word a curi-ous one. "It wasn't because she could get the merchan-dise unusually cheaply from him?"

"I've never heard of such a thing," Pauling said. "And poor Margot's dead. You can't badger her with questions."

Frayne nodded sadly. "True."

"You know, Mr. Frayne," Irene suddenly said, "what you need at the moment is some solid evidence."

Constance looked at her in astonishment. That Irene could consider solid evidence as more important at the moment than her own intuitions about the case seemed so unlikely as to be almost incredible. Then Constance realised that Irene might not be doing so. She might simply be pandering to what she regarded as an almost whimsical need in other people for plain, hard facts. Her own beliefs would remain paramount to her, but she did not mind helping the less-gifted to understand them. But it appeared that they had altered since she had last talked about them.

"There's a Biedermeier chest of drawers in the window of Conrad Greer's shop," she said. "That's solid enough, isn't it?"

Frayne gave a slight shake of his head. "I'm afraid I don't understand you."

"I mean, it's solid and heavy," she said. "It's an elegant-looking thing, but it's really quite heavy, yet when my mother and I went into the Greer shop this morning, Conrad Greer and Julie Hyland between them were moving that chest into the window. And what's your only reason for believing Julie Hyland didn't murder her sister? Isn't it only that she wouldn't have been strong enough to handle her body, get it into the car and then into the pool? But if a person's learnt how to handle heavy weights properly, they can move all sorts of things. Have you ever watched removal men handling furniture? Sometimes they're quite small men, yet between them they can carry great wardrobes and things like that up a couple of flights of stairs. And Julie had had lots of practice in the shop, so she could have carried her sister quite easily."

Constance could not stop herself interrupting. "But why should she have done that?"

"Don't you understand?" Irene said. "Julie was hopelessly in love with Conrad Greer. She had been for years, even before he had that affair with Margot and the birth of Colin. And she jumped to the conclusion when she heard Margot was here that she was going to try to get him back. So on Saturday morning, after she'd taken your order for coffee, she suddenly thought she'd go up to Riverside and tell Margot that she'd better not try to take Conrad away from her. She'd no idea then of committing murder, because, of course, she didn't know that there'd be a gun available, but she and Margot sat on the terrace talking, and we'll never know what they talked about, but perhaps Margot mocked her, saying she could get Conrad away if she chose, or threatened that she was going to expose his illegal dealing, but somehow she must have made Julie angry, and then the shooting started and there were three dead people and a gun on the floor. So she shot Margot. It must have seemed such an easy way out of her difficulties. But at just that moment Jennifer walked in. One of the odd things that's puzzled us, hasn't it, is that Jennifer didn't either bolt for her life or rush to dial 999. She seems just to have stood there, looking on and perhaps talking, and wasn't that natural if it was her own sister whom she saw committing murder?"

She paused at the sound of the front door being opened. Julie Hyland walked into the room.

Irene looked at her blankly as if the real Julie were someone whom, all the time that she had been talking, she had never really envisaged. She could easily deal with a figure that existed in her imagination, but flesh and blood upset her. She went a little pale.

"There she is," she said uneasily after the brief silence that followed Julie's entrance into the room. "I'm sure she'll confess if you show you know what she's done."

Julie stood there only for a moment, taking in the scene before her; then with the light of panic glittering wildly in her eyes, she whirled and raced from the room. Frayne snapped out a word, and the sergeant and the constable plunged after her. But Constance heard the sound of Julie's car starting up in the road before she heard the police car. But she did not think that Julie would get far.

Frayne seemed unexcited. He looked at Irene and said, "You were saying?"

"Well, I've said nearly all of it," Irene replied, "except that Julie decided she'd got to get rid of Jennifer before her conscience got the better of her and she went to the police. So as Jennifer started walking out to her car, Julie picked up the poker and hit her on the head. If she'd been really strong instead of just skilled at carrying things, I suppose she'd have killed her on the spot, but actually she only managed to knock her unconscious. Then she drove her up to the pool and drowned her there. Then, instead of walking back to the village, knowing she might be seen on the way, she came here and told Conrad Greer what she'd done. And he hid her here till just after the lunch-hour, when he knew the village would be quiet and Mrs. Crisp would have left the café, and he drove her in and she was there in time to take my mother's telephone call. About his own visit to Riverside and the chessmen, well, I think he felt he'd got to find out what was going on there, and taking the chessmen seemed a good excuse and he never dreamt they'd be easily identified as stolen. He's the kind of person who expects to be able to get away with everything."

"Thank you, Miss Lawley," the inspector said. "That's very suggestive."

"Suggestive!" she exclaimed. "Don't you believe me?"

"One's belief, unfortunately, is rarely enough to secure a conviction," he replied. "But as I said, it's suggestive. Mr. Greer, do you wish to make any comment?"

"I'm not saying anything," Conrad Greer said.

Frayne nodded, as if that were naturally to be expected.

"Then I'll just telephone for another car," he said. "It's time we were getting back to the station."

That evening Constance picked up a packet of fish and chips from the shop round the corner from the house and put it into the oven to keep warm while she and Irene drank some whisky; then, when they had had their supper, Constance rang up Mrs. Jay, whose home number she happened to know, and told her that after all, if Mrs. Jay had not already fixed them up with someone else, she would be glad to go and help the nice young couple with the dear little boy and would go to them next day if necessary.

Why she did it she was not sure. She was feeling more tired, she believed, than she had ever felt in her life, yet if she could be useful to someone who was in trouble, she thought that it might help to lift the load of depression from her more effectively than sitting at home in an empty house. She was going to miss Irene, who would be going home to her new flat next day, she supposed. In spite of the fact that while she was telephoning to Mrs. Jay a strange and dreadful noise filled the house and she knew that it was Irene practising on the French horn and that too much of it might drive her mad, she wished that the girl were staying for a little longer.

She had just sat down once more in her sitting-room and picked up her knitting, not sure if she was really in a state to concentrate on the pattern, when the doorbell rang. Wearily, she went to answer it.

A small man stood there. He was about fifty and had sandy hair which was beginning to recede from his forehead, which was high, with deep lines of thought across it, and bushy eyebrows above eyes of a clear, intense blue. His nose was short and turned up a little; his mouth was wide and smiled with singular gentleness and charm. He had a slight paunch and was wearing a wind-cheater and old, baggy trousers.

She knew what he was going to say before he said it.

"I'm Samuel," he said.

She felt sure that she was going to like him.

E. X. Ferrars, who lives in England, is the author of over fifty works of mystery and suspense, including *A Murder Too Many* and *Come To Be Killed.* She was recently given a special award by the British Crime Writers Association for continuing excellence in the mystery field.

BOOKMARK

This book was composed by Berryville Graphics Digital Composition, Berryville, Virginia, in eleven-point Renaissance, two points leaded. The display type is Compano italic. The typography and binding design are by Paul Randall Mize.